570

PHANTOM BACKFIELD

Phantom BACKFIELD

By HOWARD M. BRIER

Illustrated by Jay Hyde Barnum

jB766p

RANDOM HOUSE · NEW YORK

FOURTH PRINTING

```
TO
THE MEMORY
OF
BROADWAY
HIGH SCHOOL
```

FULL-PAGE ILLUSTRATIONS

PHANTOM BACKFIELD

LAUREL HIGH   vs.   RAVENNA HIGH

THE LINE-UP

Art Dressel	REL	Ed Pierce
Bud Radcliffe	RTL	Loren Ewan
Jack DeCourcey	RGL	Alfred Peeler
Leon Berry	C	Al Lermo
Syd Johnson	LGR	Bob Warner
Will Lanfield	LTR	Tony Farielle
Jim Pearson	LER	Dusty Moore
Lou Shafer	Q	Luke Fenner
Steve Morgan	LHR	Skiffo Drake
Ben Eskenazi	F	Vic Wade
Phil MacLain	RHL	Mert Allbrit

« « **CHAPTER ONE** » »

STEVE MORGAN, wearing the crimson-and-silver jersey of Laurel High School, walked up to the man in the striped shirt. Morgan's lips were tight, his eyes straight ahead. Standing near the referee, hands on hips and orange helmet hooked over his wrist, was Skiffo Drake, captain of the Ravenna High School eleven. Skiffo's eyes measured Steve Morgan from his unruly chestnut-colored hair to the bright black leather of his new football shoes, and his mouth twisted in a half smirk.

Steve would have preferred a more friendly meeting than this, but things had happened since last season that neither he nor Skiffo Drake had anticipated. Steve would rather have shaken hands warmly with Skiffo—would rather have patted him on the back as he had done so often at old Central High, but those days were gone forever. Circumstance had entered the picture, uncontrollable and unforeseen. It had brought consternation and even bitterness to the hearts of a thousand high school pupils. It had disrupted the faculty, and it had broken

3.

up the *Rambling Rams*, a smooth backfield combination that might have meant the city championship for old Central, and glory for Coach Hartford.

While the referee fumbled for a coin, Steve Morgan's mind was probing the past. It seemed like ages since the student body had been called into the musty assembly hall at Central High to hear the dire announcement. It seemed like ages, though it had been only the previous June.

Mr. Grosset, principal of Central High, came out on the bleak platform. The streaks of gray in his hair were more noticeable in the slanting light from the high windows. He held a sheet of paper in his hand, and it trembled as he faced the microphone. He cleared his throat.

"I am about to make an announcement that is of great concern to you who are now pupils at Central High School."

He paused. The room grew deathly quiet. Even the walls that had sheltered fifty graduation classes seemed to be crowding close, listening, as if this announcement concerned them as well as the pupils. Mr. Grosset continued.

"Because of a shift in population, and because the City of Portside is in need of a building to house technical classes for adults, the school board has decided to close

Central High School to all regular pupils starting with the fall term."

The announcement had fallen like an atom bomb, leaving the pupils stunned. Someone groaned in the back of the room, and then an undercurrent of talk that started like a whisper rose to a babble of protest.

Mr. Grosset waited patiently until the storm of rising voices had spent some of its energy. Then, with the aid of the loud-speaker, he managed to get the attention of the students once more.

"Your reaction to this announcement is quite normal," he said. "I have dreaded telling you of this decision, for it will mean making an adjustment that will not be easy. You and I love old Central High, but it has been evident for a number of years that a change would eventually come. This school once had an enrollment of twenty-three hundred. That number has dwindled to one thousand. As Portside has grown, families have moved away from the central part of the city. Business concerns have crowded in upon us. These circumstances are beyond our control."

"What about us?" someone cried from the balcony. "What will they do with us?"

"I was coming to that," Principal Grosset said. "There are eight other high schools in Portside. These other schools have newer buildings. They are not over-crowded. Our district will be divided among four of the adjacent districts. Many of you will go to Laurel High."

"Never!"

It was a cry of defiance, and it echoed the feeling of a thousand young people who had worked their hearts out to defeat Laurel on every field of sport. There was no laughter at the sudden outburst. Instead, a mutter of agreement passed through the room. Laurel High? Never! How could the fighting *Rams* of Central High change into *Hawks* overnight? How could the athletes of old Central pull off their purple sweaters and don the crimson-and-silver of Laurel High? These two schools had been deadly rivals. Ravenna High, maybe, or Hilltop, but Laurel—never!

"There will be some," Principal Grosset had said, "who will have reasonable grounds for not wishing to attend certain high schools. The school board will make provision for such pupils. Members of the junior class who will be seniors next fall will be allowed to attend the school of their choice. Others will attend the school specified by the district revision."

The assembly had not lasted long. It had closed with the ringing of the bell at three fifteen. The pupils shuffled out, still muttering. Someone started the chant —"Laurel High, NEVER!"—and the words echoed through the crowded corridors of the old building and bounced back and forth among the high lockers that lined the walls.

The referee found the coin.

"What do you take, Ravenna?" he asked.

"Heads," Skiffo Drake mumbled.

The silver coin spun in the air and landed heads up.

"We'll defend the west goal," Skiffo Drake said.

The referee turned to Steve Morgan.

"We'll receive," Steve said.

The two players started away.

"Just a minute," the referee called. "Haven't you forgotten something? How about shaking hands?"

Steve Morgan extended his hand first. Skiffo Drake shook it in a perfunctory way. The handshake was a mere formality.

Morgan's teeth were digging into his underlip as he walked back to his teammates. Thoughts were elbowing one another in his mind. This was not right, this animosity between himself and Skiffo Drake. Last year they were the best of friends; this year they were enemies. Last year they were playing together with clock-like precision, tossing laterals, running interference; this year they were facing each other across hostile lines, wearing different jerseys, fighting for new schools.

Where were the *Rambling Rams* of last year—the backfield that was going places? Sports writers had hailed them as the answer to a coach's dream. Running, passing, kicking—each one of the four was a threat. Give them another year, the grandstand quarterbacks said, and the city title would be in the bag. Coach Hartford had nursed them along from freshmen. There was stocky Larry Bowman. He was playing for Hilltop High. There was Big Bill Toner, former fullback for old Central. He had a new job this year packing the ball for Wallingford High. And here was Skiffo Drake, captain of the Ravenna *Bruins*. Larry Bowman, Big Bill Toner, Skiffo Drake, and Steve Morgan—a neat combination. And now they were scattered to the four winds. A phantom backfield!

The cheering in the stands was a dull rumble in Steve Morgan's ears. No doubt Larry Bowman and Big Bill Toner were up in the crowd watching this opener. What were they thinking as they waited for the kick-off? Steve ran his hand through his hair and fitted his helmet in place—a silver helmet this time, instead of gold.

Coach Hartford, who had been moved to Laurel High when old Central had been disbanded, called his players together. In the huddle they clasped hands, and the coach's words were intended to give confidence to a squad that had demonstrated through five long weeks of practice that it lacked confidence.

"You fellows can take Ravenna High," he said, "if you keep your heads up, and if you hang onto the ball. I can't help you much after the whistle blows. For sixty minutes you have to play football. If you play it smart you can win, and more power to you."

Hartford could feel the tension of this squad. A third of his team had played for Central High last season. The rest were holdovers from previous Laurel teams. There was no bond between these players, no feeling of unity. They were as nervous as young colts, as unpredictable as lightning.

From experience Hartford knew that a football team had to work like a machine. It was made up of component parts, and each part moved in a certain groove, had a definite job to perform. If the parts failed to function properly, the machine stalled. That could happen to this Laurel High School team. It could happen with a fumble, or an intercepted pass, or a clipping penalty. It could happen in a hundred different ways.

As the huddle broke up and the players moved into their positions to receive the kickoff, Steve Morgan thought of the meeting in the Beanery after Principal Grosset's assembly announcement. It had seemed as if the entire student body were trying to shove its way into the stuffy little eating place across from the school.

"They can't do this to us," Skiffo Drake had shouted in the Beanery. He was standing on a stool near the counter. The room was filled with the odor of frying hamburgers. Skiffo had to shout to be heard above the commotion. "I tell you, they can't do this to us." He ran long, bony fingers through his hair. His large nose was inflamed from a cold, and his eyes had a feverish gleam.

"We got to organize. We got powerful alumni. We'll go to the school board . . . the super'tendent. We'll get our folks to fight. We'll get the P. T. A. behind us. They can't do this to us." Skiffo struck a pose with his fists clenched above his head. "There's only one thing for us to do, gang. We'll strike!"

"You tell 'em, Skiffo," a classmate shouted. A mutter passed through the restless crowd. "Skiffo's right. We'll strike! We'll strike!"

Penny Carson, who was a member of the yell team, and who was always bubbling over with enthusiasm for old Central, was edging her way through the crowd. Her cheeks were flushed. She had lost a bobby pin in the jam so that a lock of auburn hair hung down over one eye. "Skiffo!" she shrieked. "Help me up there, Skiffo. We have to put this over."

Penny's enthusiasm was catching. She soon had the crowd giving the old Central war chant. The yell sounded muffled in those cramped quarters, but the words were vibrant with emotion. *"Fight 'em, Rams, Fight 'em! Fight 'em, Rams, Fight 'em!"*

When the yell was over there was a moment of hushed silence. Then Penny's voice, shrill with defiance, rang out.

"Are we going to let them close old Central High?"

"No!" bellowed the belligerent crowd.

"Are we going to let them shove us around like sheep?"

"No!" The cry was more determined.

"Are we going to let them kill the old Purple and Gold spirit?"

"No! No! No!"

"Well, what are we going to do about it?"

"Strike!" the gang shouted. "Strike!"

"Okay. Tomorrow is Friday. Tomorrow we don't go to classes. Right?"

"Right! We're all with you, Penny!"

Skiffo, his cheeks ballooned from a generous bite of hamburger, was ready to take over. He helped Penny from the stool and clambered up in her place.

"Okay, gang. This strike has to go over one hundred per cent. The papers will play it up. There'll be an awful smell, but we got to stick together. One for all . . . all for Central."

The crowd took up the phrase. "One for all . . . all for Central," it chanted.

It was some time before Skiffo could get attention.

"Quiet!" Skiffo shouted, holding one hand up as he had seen dictators do in the newsreels. "Quiet, you birds."

Those who could hear turned to the jabbering students behind them. "Pipe down," they shouted. "Listen to Skiffo."

Gradually the noise subsided.

"I've played three years of football for old Central," Skiffo said, "and there are others like me. We don't want to play for any other school. We have our hooks on that title next year, and every team in the city knows it. We can't let them break up our combination. I'm going to call on some of the other players in this gang just so you can see how they feel about it."

Skiffo looked over the crowd.

"There's Larry Bowman. What do you say, Larry?"

"I'm all for striking," Larry shouted. "Nobody asked us for our opinion. We're getting a raw deal, if you ask me."

There was a shout of approval from the crowd.

"And here's Big Bill Toner over here," Skiffo said, pointing. "Do you want to play for Laurel next year?"

"Do I look crazy?" Big Bill replied. "I wouldn't play for Laurel if it was the last school on earth."

"Okay," Skiffo shouted, as the spontaneous cry of agreement died away. "There's another fellow here who ought to say a few words. He's way over there in the corner. Come on up, Steve Morgan, and tell the gang what you think."

Steve hesitated.

"We want Morgan," someone yelled. The other students took up the cry.

Reluctantly, Steve moved toward the stool. The crowd opened a path for him. Skiffo stepped down, and Steve Morgan took his place.

"You fellows aren't going to like what I have to say," Steve started.

The crowd, slightly taken aback, grew quiet.

"Like Skiffo here, I've played three years of football

for old Central. Nobody loves the old school any more than I do. My dad and my mother both went to Central, and my older brother was a three-letter man a few years ago. That's why Central means a lot in our family."

Steve paused for breath, and the crowd waited expectantly.

"Our school is an old school," Steve continued. "Its traditions started before any of us were born, and they'll be remembered as long as any of us live. It was a privilege to go to old Central, but you and I have seen this change coming. We had hoped that it wouldn't come until we had graduated, but it didn't work out that way."

The crowd, sensing the switch in Steve Morgan's talk, grew restless. "We want Skiffo!" someone shouted, but Steve continued to hold the stool.

"If we strike tomorrow," Steve said, "the people of Portside will think we can't take it."

"Who wants to take it?" a wild-eyed sophomore shouted.

Steve ignored the remark.

"If we strike tomorrow we'll be giving old Central a dirty deal."

"How do you figure? The school board's giving us a dirty deal." It was Blink Kennedy shouting defiance.

Blink Kennedy was the best dancer in school, but no athlete.

"Quit thinking about yourself," Steve said, his voice rising. "Think about the school—its reputation. Old Central deserves to go out with colors flying. If we strike tomorrow we'll be deserting our school. Everybody in Portside will be watching us, and they'll judge our school by how we act. I'll be in my classes tomorrow because I'm going to stay loyal to old Central right up to the end."

Steve got down from the stool, and Skiffo glared at him.

"Beautiful speech," Skiffo muttered, sarcastically. "What's the matter, Steve? Gone chicken?"

Blink Kennedy pushed through the crowd. "So I'm thinking of myself, am I? Take that!" He swung at Steve, but Morgan ducked. Blink's fist brushed the side of his head. Steve whirled and caught Blink on the chin with a well-aimed blow. Blink staggered back, groggy, and he was glad that others stepped in to stop the fight.

Skiffo clambered back on the stool, tried to get the attention of the crowd.

"Pay no attention to Steve," he shouted. "We got to get organized."

But the crowd was breaking up, moving away in little

muttering groups. Skiffo found himself with only a handful of followers, and even those who had been most rabid had lost some of their enthusiasm. Steve Morgan's speech had dampened the fire that had burned within them.

The next day, when the strike failed to materialize, Skiffo Drake resolved to even the score with Steve Morgan if it was the last thing he ever did.

Steve Morgan was in the left-half spot ready to receive. The Laurel team was spread out over the east end of the field, nervously awaiting the referee's whistle. Skiffo Drake was placing the ball in position on the forty-yard line. The Ravenna *Bruins* were lined up on the thirty-five. Skiffo moved back, glancing from left to right to see that his teammates were on side. He raised his hand. The referee looked at Steve Morgan. Steve signaled that his men were ready. The official's whistle sounded shrill, and far away. The orange-clad *Bruin* line moved forward with Skiffo's kick. The ball rose in the air, sailed end-over-end, straight down the field to the waiting arms of Eskenazi, Laurel fullback. The game was on.

Eskenazi took the ball on the ten-yard line, and started down the center of the field. Steve moved in fast to help form the interference. He collided with a *Bruin* tackle on the thirty-yard stripe, and found himself the center of a whirling mass of arms and legs. Eskenazi had piled

up right over him and the ball was down on the thirty-two.

The Laurel team went into a huddle. Lou Shafer, quarterback, looked his men over. "Okay," he said. "Number six."

Number six was an off-tackle play, with Steve carrying the ball. There was little deception to the play, but if the tackle boxed the opposing lineman in, and if the interference took the end out, it was good for a few yards. Shafer was playing it safe, planning to feel out the Ravenna line.

The Laurel men were down in position, the center over the ball. Steve, Eskenazi, and Phil MacLain, right half, were ready for the shift.

"One . . . two . . . three. . . ." The four men moved to the left, three fancy steps with their heads up, and then went into the crouch, hands on knees.

"Hip!"

The ball came direct to Steve. He wrapped his arms around it, and was moving fast toward the left sideline. Phil took the end in a rolling block, and Steve cut in. There was a hole off tackle—not too wide, but wide enough. Head down, Steve shot through, legs driving. He was past the scrimmage line, and was straightening up for an open field run, when Skiffo Drake hit him low from the left. At the same instant, Wade, the Ravenna fullback, caught him around the shoulders, and Steve doubled up like a jackknife. He hit the ground hard, and he felt a thud under his elbow. The ball shot out of his arms. He saw it bounce away, and he was powerless to get it. The Ravenna center pounced on the ball, and the referee's whistle sounded.

A sickening wave passed over Steve. He had fumbled on the first running play of the game, and the ball was in Ravenna's possession on their own thirty-five-yard line.

As Skiffo Drake released his hold on Morgan's legs and scrambled to his feet, he looked at the Laurel halfback without any sign of friendship. "Thanks for the break," he said. "You never fumbled like that for old Central."

Steve walked away without making a reply. He felt that the eyes of every Laurel rooter were on him as he moved to his position on defense.

The Ravenna stands were wild with excitement. Their cry rang out. "We want a touchdown! We want a touchdown!"

The Laurel pupils were hushed, stunned by the sudden turn of events.

Across the scrimmage line the Ravenna *Bruins* were in a huddle. They came out of it with the easy rhythm of a well-coached team. Skiffo Drake was at right half. He glanced across the crouching line as the quarterback called the shift.

"One . . . two . . . three . . . hike!"

The ball went in a fast spiral to Skiffo. He was running to his left, with three men for interference. One of the Ravenna backfield men took Art Dressel out with a neat block. Skiffo cut in, found himself past the scrimmage line. Steve Morgan headed for him, and as Steve dove for the tackle, Skiffo spun around. Steve felt the elusive hips wrench from his grip. Five yards more and Lou Shafer hit Skiffo, brought him down on the twenty-two-yard line.

Twelve yards on one play. It gave Ravenna a first down. The referee motioned to the head linesman to move the chain. Skiffo trotted back to the Ravenna huddle with the cockiness of a bird dog. He had made Steve look silly on that tackle.

"Here we go! Here we go!" The cry came from the Ravenna stands, and it carried across the field in wild exuberance.

"No you don't! No you don't!" The answering chant came from Laurel, but it carried less conviction. Laurel was on the spot. The game was only two minutes old, and already Ravenna was a threat.

The next play was a quick pass. Fenner, the quarterback, faded and leaped into the air. He shot the ball like a bullet to the Ravenna end who was streaking across in the slot. Eskenazi hit the end on the sixteen, and brought him down.

It was second down and four yards to go for Ravenna.

On the next play, Wade, the Ravenna fullback, picked up three yards off tackle.

The Laurel line, expecting a quarterback sneak, bunched toward the center, but Ravenna fooled them with a pass into the flat. It was Skiffo to Moore, and it placed the ball on the five-yard line. Goal to go.

Laurel called for time-out, hoping that during the breather Ravenna would lose some of its drive.

Steve had a sinking feeling as he lined up for the next play. He felt responsible for this set-up, and the deathly quiet in the Laurel stands only lowered his spirit.

He watched the *Bruin* players come out of the huddle, confident, alert. Skiffo was in position, hands on his knees, the trace of a grin on his lips. Skiffo always was a cocksure player. Even at old Central he had played with dash and an air of easy unconcern. Skiffo's jauntiness had not seemed so bad when Steve had been playing in the same backfield with him. Now it was a flaunt, a dare. It seemed to say, "I'm the great Skiffo Drake. Try and stop me."

Skiffo was not easy to stop. Laurel found that out on

the next play. Skiffo took it in stride, ran wide around end, and when he cut in near the sideline he collided with Eskenazi on the one-yard line.

The referee brought the ball out fifteen yards from the sideline. Ravenna tried a line smash, with Wade carrying the ball. He hit a stone wall, and the ball was still on the one-yard marker when the referee straightened up.

The *Bruins* had two downs to push it over, but Skiffo Drake needed only one. On the next play he went over standing up. The Ravenna team had opened a hole in the Laurel line, and Drake spun through on his toes.

"Like a ballet dancer," Steve Morgan thought, and he almost expected Skiffo to take a bow.

Ravenna made the try-for-point, and the scoreboard recorded in black numerals: RAVENNA 7, LAUREL 0.

CHAPTER TWO

COACH HARTFORD sent a substitute in for Steve Morgan after the touchdown. Steve expected a reprimand for the fumble, but the coach simply nodded him to the bench.

Steve pulled the hood of a parka over his head, and sat down. He felt desperately lonely. He wanted to talk to the players crowding on either side, but they seemed like strangers to him. What could he talk about? The fumble? It would seem like an alibi if he said that someone punched the ball out of his arms. He dug his cleats into the sod and said nothing.

He thought of the long hours of training, the grueling scrimmages on the muddy practice field until darkness had blotted out the ball and the players. He thought of Coach Hartford during practice, crouching behind the backfield, wheedling, urging, driving his men in an effort to mold a football team out of raw material that refused to be molded. There was something wrong with this Laurel team, and it was not difficult for Steve to figure out where the trouble lay. It had been fairly obvious from the start of the season. The members of this team were not working together. They were individualists, looking out for their own interests. They were not pulling for each other. The feeling of unity that had been uppermost at old Central was missing at Laurel High. There was no horseplay in the locker room, and after scrimmage the fellows never sang in the showers. Steve had a feeling that Laurel could never win football games with players who would not sing in the showers.

After the touchdown, Ravenna had kicked off to Laurel, and Lou Shafer had run the ball back to the thirty-yard line. In three downs Laurel gained only seven yards, and Eskenazi kicked on the fourth.

It looked like another march for the *Bruins*. They pounded holes in the Laurel line, and carried the ball off tackle and around the ends until it was first down on Laurel's twenty-two.

Coach Hartford was nervous. He paced up and down the sidelines like a sea captain in stormy weather.

Skiffo Drake dropped back to pass. Moore and Ed Pierce, *Bruin* ends, were in the clear. It looked like a set-up, but Radcliffe, the Laurel tackle, had drifted through the line, and he was on top of Skiffo before he could get the ball away. It put Ravenna back on the thirty-two, and it seemed like a break for Laurel.

Steve Morgan hugged the bench, biting his lip. He tried to account for his feelings. He should have felt elated that Skiffo had been caught so far behind his line, but there was no elation in his feelings. Instead, he felt a little sorry for Skiffo. That was not right. Steve ran his hand across his eyes and closed them tight. His thoughts were all mixed.

Ravenna lost the ball on downs after their long march. Eskenazi kicked on the third down, and the ball was back in midfield.

The second quarter was a seesaw affair, with most of the playing in Laurel territory. Somehow the crimson team managed to stave off another touchdown. At the half the score was still 7 to 0 in favor of Ravenna.

In the locker room during the half Coach Hartford spent most of his time tending to injuries. As he taped Leon Berry's ankle, he turned to Steve.

"How you feeling, Morgan?"

"I'm all right, Coach. That fumble . . ."

"Forget it." Hartford's words were not harsh. "You were nervous. Don't let them punch the ball out of your arms. Hang onto it."

Then Hartford had noticed. Steve felt better.

When the two teams lined up for the second half, Steve Morgan was back in his position.

Wade, Ravenna fullback, took the kick and powered his way back to the forty. Skiffo made eight off tackle, and Steve Morgan brought him down.

As Skiffo got slowly to his feet he lingered near Steve.

"Like to make a speech?" he said, sarcasm in his voice. "With a little oratory you might get them to close Ravenna High."

Steve stood with his hands on his hips and watched Skiffo walk back to the *Bruin* huddle. There were things he wanted to say to Skiffo but he knew this was neither the time nor the place.

Somehow his mind went back to an incident that had happened during the last week of school at old Central. It was an incident that brought color surging to his cheeks whenever it was recalled.

It was Monday evening, and Steve had his work spread out on the dining-room table with the idea of studying for an examination. To his surprise he discovered that he had left his history book at school. There was only one thing to do—make a trip to the school to see if he could get the book.

"Do you think the building will be open?" his mother had asked.

"There'll be a janitor around somewhere. I'll get in."

It was dark when Steve reached Central High, but a

light was burning in the second-floor study hall. Steve tossed a pebble against the window and attracted the attention of the janitor. The window was opened, and Steve explained his trouble.

"Just a minute," the janitor said. "I'll let you in the front door."

The janitor waited at the door while Steve went to his locker and secured the book. It took him several minutes, and when he left the janitor locked the door after him.

The next morning Steve was called from his biology class. Mr. Grosset was waiting for him in his private office. He had a sober look on his face as he motioned Steve to a chair.

"I understand you were in the building last night," Mr. Grosset said.

"Yes, sir," Steve replied. "I came for a book."

"We had an unfortunate experience here last night. The trophy case was broken open, and someone stole the All-city Cup."

"Yes, I heard about . . ." suddenly Steve gulped. "You . . . you don't suspect that I . . ."

"No, Steve," the principal replied. "I don't suspect you. But I thought you might be able to shed a little light on the disappearance of the trophy. Did you see anyone prowling about the premises when you were here?"

"No, sir. If I had I surely would have reported it."

"I'm certain of it. Now I want you to keep your eyes and ears open. If you get any information let me know at once."

"Yes, sir. I will."

How the story got around, Steve never knew, but before the day was over it was common talk that Steve had been questioned in Mr. Grosset's office about the missing trophy. An office girl, with ears tuned to gossip, might have been responsible. However it got out, the harm was done. No amount of explanation could ever quite remove the stigma of suspicion. Until the mystery was solved, Steve felt that his name would always be linked with the disappearance of the cup.

It was difficult to get his mind back on the football game.

Ravenna had possession of the ball most of the third quarter. They pulled everything out of the bag in an effort to score, but Laurel managed to hold them. It was generally an individual player, making a bid for glory, who stopped the Ravenna push.

Phil MacLain stopped them late in the third quarter. Ravenna was heading for a touchdown. They passed from the thirty-yard line, and MacLain intercepted the ball on the eight. Eskenazi had to kick from behind the goal line, and when the quarter ended Ravenna had the ball again on the Laurel forty-five.

The fourth quarter was different. With the teams switched, and with the *Bruins* marching for the west goal, their luck seemed to change.

Laurel was powerless to stop the big orange-clad team in their fourth-quarter drive, and this time Ravenna punched it over in a series of line bucks. Wade made the touchdown, but it was Skiffo Drake and Allbrit who paved the way for him. The scoreboard read 13 to 0, and the minute hand on the big clock was swinging around the dial.

The game went on to a dogged finish, with the Laurel team moving through a fog that never seemed to lift.

In the locker room after the game Steve Morgan undressed in silence. He felt depressed. He looked around at his sweat-streaked teammates. Every face was covered with gloom. He wrapped a towel around his stocky body, and started for the showers. He found several of the fellows ahead of him. There were Eskenazi, Lou Shafer, Phil MacLain. There was Syd Johnson, left guard, with a purple shiner that reached to his cheekbone. They stood hunched in the showers like naked scarecrows in a rainstorm.

Steve stood for a moment in the doorway and watched the steam curl from the floor like smoke. He found an unused shower, and adjusted the water. As he started to lather his arms and chest, he broke into the words of a familiar song.

"Oh—give me a home where the buffalo roam . . ."

Lou Shafer and Eskenazi stopped their bathing and stared at Steve in surprise.

"Where the deer and the antelope play . . ."

From the far end of the shower room, DeCourcey, right guard, joined in with an uncertain tenor.

"Where seldom is heard a discouraging word . . ."

Shafer, Eskenazi, and Pearson were in on the next line.

"And the skies are not cloudy all day."

"Altogether now," Steve shouted.

The harmony that poured forth from the shower room was sweet music to Coach Hartford. He had a vague hunch that before the season was over Laurel High would have a football team.

CHAPTER THREE

STEVE MORGAN moved up the wide cement walk that led to Laurel High. It was Monday morning. A cold, wind-driven rain was slanting down from a murky sky. Lights were on in most of the classrooms for it was almost time for the bell. The building looked like a warm haven on this stormy morning, but Steve walked reluctantly. He was timing his arrival so that he would not have to loiter about the halls and perhaps suffer some embarrassing moments. It would be difficult to explain that fumble on the first play of the game with Ravenna High. Coach Hartford had seen the Ravenna player punch the ball out of Morgan's arms, but Steve felt sure that the crowd in the stands had not. They would blame him for part of the defeat. He could avoid embarrassment by arriving late, but he had no desire to avoid responsibility. Steve knew that he was partly to blame. He should have hung onto the ball.

The Sunday papers had given Skiffo Drake plenty of praise for the part he had played in the Ravenna victory.

One sports writer had said, "The disbanding of old Central High did not seem to hamper Skiffo Drake's ability on the gridiron. He displayed the same brilliant dash for the Ravenna *Bruins* that made him outstanding last year for the Purple and Gold. If this continues throughout the season Skiffo will dance right into a backfield spot on the Portside All-city team."

To make the All-city in Portside was a double honor. It not only meant recognition for superior ability in the largest city in the state, it meant an opportunity to play in a post-season game against an All-state eleven selected from the smaller cities outside of Portside.

Steve Morgan had dreamed of making the All-city, but in his sophomore and junior years his name had not been mentioned as a possibility. Skiffo Drake had made the second squad during the previous season at old Central, but the All-city coach had more backfield material than he could use, so Skiffo had warmed the bench during the post-season battle. This year it would be different. Skiffo was a senior, and already they were building him up for a position on the team.

Steve did not begrudge Skiffo any recognition he could win. But there were times when Steve longed to merit some of the top honors that went with success on the gridiron. Each year he had given the game everything he had, but when the awards were passed out other players won the inspirational trophies, and Steve was handed another felt letter to add to the collection on the wall above his bed.

As he walked up the slippery steps to Laurel High, Steve could not help feeling that the disbanding of old Central had made a great difference in his life. Though he was a senior, and knew that he would graduate in June, he felt almost like a freshman at Laurel. He had elected to come to Laurel because it was the school closest to his home. The building was new. The halls and classrooms were different. Most of the faculty members were strangers. That would not have been the case if the school board had not closed Central High. There everyone knew him. The underclassmen looked up to him. The teachers nodded to him in the halls. He felt at home. There was something about old Central that got into your blood, made you feel a part of the school itself. It was a feeling that he had not experienced at Laurel. After five weeks in the new school he still felt like a visitor when he pushed through the heavy doors and entered the wide central hall.

The clock over the auditorium entrance pointed to 8:40. The warning bell had rung, and Steve had five minutes to get to his chemistry class. This was just as he had planned it. Other pupils were hurrying through the halls, too busy to talk. Steve headed for the locker room. He would get his notebook, his chem text, and his trig book. During second-period study he would go over his trig lesson. His thoughts were on his schedule for the day. Third period he had United States History. That was a cinch. He had read the assignment twice the day before. He reached his locker, and automatically shoved the key in place.

"Hiya, Steve!"

Steve Morgan looked around, surprised. The greeting had come from a little red-haired freshman two lockers down.

"Hello," Steve replied, still surprised. He had never seen this boy before.

"That was a swell game you played against Ravenna." The freshman's eyes were gleaming with appreciation, and the freckles that arched over his pug nose were squeezed together from his broad grin.

"Not too hot," Steve said, groping for his trig book and trying to hang his jacket on the hook at the same time.

"We got a team, Steve." The freshman was leaning against the locker, oblivious to the march of time. "Sure, we booted one game, but what's one game among friends? We're going to take Hilltop next week. They'll think it's another attack on Iwo Jima."

Steve straightened up, ran his fingers through his hair for lack of a comb.

"Aren't you afraid you'll be late for first period?" Steve asked.

"Not me," the freshman replied. "My algebra teacher doesn't put her glasses on until 9:05. She can't see across her desk without her glasses. I'm just a dark blur slippin' through the door."

"I'm not so lucky," Steve replied. "My chem teacher has good eyes. Be seeing you."

"Remember what I said," the freshman called after him. "Friday we take Hilltop."

Steve ran up the stairs two at a time. He reached the door of his chemistry class just as the bell was ringing. Mr. Baker was calling the roll.

"Steve Morgan?" the teacher said, without looking up.

"Here." Steve grinned sheepishly as he slid into his seat. Syd Johnson, his chem partner, was already in place.

"Thought you weren't going to make it," Syd said, in a low tone.

"So did I," Steve replied. "A frosh cornered me in the locker room, and I couldn't break away."

"One of your fans?"

"I should have a fan after last Saturday's game."

"Still brooding over that fumble? Forget it. As Lady Macbeth so aptly put it, 'What's done cannot be undone,' end of quote."

"Syd!" It was Mr. Baker looking up from his desk. "The bell has rung. Will you please stop talking?"

"I was just quoting Shakespeare."

"And what does Mr. Shakespeare have to say about the quantitative analysis of organic compounds?"

Mr. Baker switched bits of conversation to the field of chemistry with the adeptness of a radio announcer going into a sales talk.

Syd was more than willing to forget Shakespeare. Experience had taught him that he was no match for Mr. Baker when it came to repartee. But Mr. Baker was not content to let the matter drop.

"Syd," he said, "being a student of Shakespeare, perhaps you can define a soliloquy for the class."

Syd had a feeling that he was being trapped, but he blundered through with a definition. "A soliloquy," he said, "is when one person gets up and does a lot of talking all by himself—sort of a monologue, like when Brutus buried Caesar."

"Good," Mr. Baker enthused. "Now, Syd, I want you to come in front of the class and give us a little soliloquy on the subject of Organic Compounds."

"Okay," Syd muttered. "I lose." He shuffled to the front of the room and faced his grinning classmates.

Steve felt sorry for him, but he knew that Syd would come through in a pinch. He always did on the football field. He was a dependable guard, and Coach Hartford never worried about his spot in the line. The soliloquy he delivered on Organic Compounds was deserving of a "B" grade in Mr. Baker's class book.

"Very good," Mr. Baker mumbled. "Hmmmmm! Very good. And now Steve, can you tell us . . ."

Somehow Steve got through his chemistry recitation, but during second period in the study hall he found himself gazing out of the window, across the wide front lawn to the practice field in the adjacent block. It was still raining. The field was deserted save for some seagulls that seemed to find satisfaction in parading across the muddy flat.

With a little stretch of the imagination those seagulls became football players in Steve Morgan's mind. It was hard to concentrate on trigonometry with a football game going on out there in the rain.

The period was half over when Steve noticed someone coming up the aisle. It was the little freshman who had confronted him in the locker room before school. The freshman was on the way to the dictionary stand at the rear of the room. He hesitated for a moment in front of Steve, and then as he passed he dropped a folded slip of notebook paper on the desk.

Steve opened the sheet and found a note written in a bold, backhand scrawl.

Steve Morgan—You are my unanimous choice for left halfback on the Portside All-city team. You are going to show those wise guys who write sports just how football is played. I predict you make two touchdowns for Laurel High when we play Hilltop next Friday. The final score will be Laurel 21, Hilltop 12.

Your friend,

YOGI ZIMMERMAN

Steve glanced around. The little freshman was grinning at him from the dictionary stand. Steve held up his hand with the forefinger touching the thumb. The freshman nodded assurance. Steve felt good. He had one friend at Laurel High.

That afternoon, during the practice scrimmage, Steve was the sparkplug of the first eleven. Whenever Lou Shafer handed him the ball he was good for six, eight, or ten yards. He tore the second-team line to ribbons, and when the play called for a pass he heaved the slippery pigskin into the hands of a receiver with such accuracy that Coach Hartford's squinting eyes gleamed with a new light.

Eskenazi, Laurel's 180-pound fullback, and Phil Mac-Lain, scatback who played in the right-half position, seemed to catch Steve Morgan's spirit. They made the second team look silly. Even the linemen were clicking. They opened holes that were big enough for a jeep to pass through. On one such play Steve moved so fast that his feet went out from under him. He slid six yards through a puddle of water, and when he got up his face was plastered with mud.

Syd Johnson, who had taken a roller-coaster ride through the same puddle, scrambled to his feet. His football pants were soaking wet, his cleats were caked with an inch of mud, and his helmet was cocked on one side while a broken strap dangled under his dripping chin.

"Now we're rolling," he mumbled, as he made his way back to the huddle with Steve.

"You mean sliding." Steve grinned. His teeth gleamed in startling contrast to his dirt-streaked face.

"Why couldn't we play like this against Ravenna?"

" 'What's done cannot be undone,' " Steve quoted, in his best Shakespearean voice.

"Okay," Syd said. "Rub it in. I took my beating in chemistry. I'll never stick my neck out in Baker's class again."

It was a long practice session on this drizzly, wet Monday afternoon. Coach Hartford kept pounding away on line drives, but now and then he called for a pass.

"Got to learn to handle a wet ball," he said, "and I mean *handle* it. Lot of teams are world beaters on a dry field, but they crack up in the mud. The kind of team I want can play football in fair weather or foul. Keep your tail down, DeCourcey. A guard plays close to the ground. And you, Dressel, you're dragging your feet on that short pass. You have to move fast. The ball isn't going to hang around and wait for you. You have to be there when it comes."

Hartford kept changing the second-team players, but the first team remained the same. It was the longest scrimmage session of the season. Four o'clock arrived. Five o'clock. At five-thirty it was so dark even the quarterback couldn't see the ball.

"All right," Hartford said. "Twice around the track, and showers."

Tired, drenched, sore, the players started trotting around the cinder oval. They were too weary to wisecrack; too exhausted to complain.

In the showers Lou Shafer found himself next to Steve.

"How you holding up?" he asked.

"Not bad. Only trouble is my knees want to fold up."

"Was Hartford a slave driver like this when he was at Central High?"

"He used to ride us pretty hard when we lost a game. By the end of the season we were all for him."

"I like the guy, personally, but he sure cuts out a day's work for small pay."

"You'll feel well paid after we take Hilltop next Friday."

"What makes you think we're going to take Hilltop?"

"A little freshman told me."

"You feelin' all right, Steve? You sure you didn't get bumped on the head, or something?"

"Not a bump. In fact, I can even tell you what the score will be."

"You *don't* say!" Shafer exaggerated the words. He turned to the others in the shower room. "Silence, everybody! Important announcement! Steve Morgan will now tell us the score of the Laurel-Hilltop game. Quiet, you birds!"

"The score . . ." Steve said, repeating the words for emphasis, "the score will be LAUREL 21, HILLTOP 12."

"Hurray!" Art Dressel shouted. "We win! Nice game, gang. We sure made those guys look sick."

No one had noticed Coach Hartford in the doorway. It was his voice that interrupted the cheering.

"You fellows play pretty good football in the showers. Let's hope some of it carries over onto the field."

CHAPTER FOUR

LAUREL HELD a pep assembly on Thursday for the game with Hilltop. Steve attended more out of curiosity than loyalty. He remembered the football rallies they had held at Central High before each game. At old Central the auditorium had been used for a study hall during the day, and when the entire student body was packed into the room it was filled to overflowing. Pupils sat on the desks, the window sills, anywhere that they could get a seat. The crowded room had made the rallies seem more personal.

Here at Laurel High there was a seat for everybody— not just a study-hall desk, but a regular auditorium seat. The stage was big, with red velvet curtains, and a proscenium arch as sweeping as those found in large city theaters. The entire band could be seated on the stage, and there was still room for stunts, and yell leaders, and speakers. Footlights and powerful spotlights from a projection booth high in the balcony gave the stage a theatrical appearance that could never have been achieved at old Central. But something was lacking. At least that was the feeling Steve Morgan had. When the pupils cheered it seemed purposeless. The school was too big, too new to have traditions trailing off into the past. There was no ivy growing on the walls, no famous alumni to come back to tell of the *good old days*—no background.

The assembly started with the pledge to the flag, and then the band played *The Star Spangled Banner*. It was a big band of seventy pieces, and the music sounded good. Steve noted with a little pride that there were several Central High band members on the stage. Jake Logan, who played the trombone, was up there. Jake had been in Comp II with Steve at old Central. But for the most part the players were strangers to Steve. This was not his band. This band would never play *For The Glory of The Rams* the way the old Central band had played it. Steve could remember the thrill he got when that music came booming out over the gridiron. It made a fellow want to dig in. It made a fellow want to win.

The Laurel yell team came trotting out in new crimson sweaters and white trousers with crimson stripes down the side. They looked flashy on the stage, but they evidently needed practice, for they got mixed up on the first two yells and had to start over. The third yell went smoothly, but it was a simple yell, and there was not much chance for a mistake.

> *Go get 'em, Laurel High, Go get 'em!*
> *Go get 'em, Laurel High, Go get 'em!*
> *Hit 'em high, Laurel High, Hit 'em low!*
> *Let's go, Laurel High, Let's go!*

Steve tried yelling with the rest, but he felt self-conscious. Somehow he couldn't muster the same volume that he had given to the old Central yells. His efforts were half-hearted.

After the yell team had disappeared in the wings, a girl came out on the stage. She approached the microphone with plenty of assurance. Steve sat up in his seat, for he recognized Penny Carson. Penny had been prominent at Central High, but she had not spoken to Steve since the episode in the Beanery when she and Skiffo Drake had tried to stir up the protest strike. Because Steve had been largely responsible for discouraging the strike, she held it against him personally. She had come to Laurel High against her wishes. Now Penny Carson was going to talk. The trace of a smile showed at the corner of Steve's mouth, and he listened attentively.

"We are going to play a football game tomorrow," Penny said. Her voice was low, pleasing. "We want to win that game. That goes for those of us who will be up in the stands as well as the players on the field. We have a good team. We have a good coach. We have a good student body. When we all start working together there isn't a team in the city that can stop us."

A cheer started in the balcony, and was picked up by the older pupils on the lower floor. Penny looked toward the balcony and smiled.

"There is the start of a real school spirit," she said. "We upperclassmen at Laurel High can learn something from the freshmen. They have come to Laurel High without any prejudices, or split loyalties. They have confidence in what Laurel High can accomplish."

Steve thought of Yogi Zimmerman and his faith in the team. Penny was right about the freshmen.

"We who came from old Central," Penny continued, "want to thank the pupils of Laurel High for the fine way you received us. It was not easy for us to make the change, and it will be even more difficult for us to build up a new loyalty to replace the old. But that's what we are trying to do. And with your help I am sure we will succeed. Now we have a job to do on Friday. The *Rams* from old Central, and the *Hawks* from Laurel High can do it together. That job is to beat Hilltop. How about it?"

The response this time was spontaneous. When the cheering had quieted down Penny continued.

"And now we have a surprise for you. We have invited one of the Hilltop players to give a little talk about the game tomorrow. This boy was a star football player at old Central before he transferred to Hilltop. He is really among friends, but he doesn't know it. I would like to introduce Larry Bowman, quarterback for Hilltop."

Larry Bowman, wearing soiled cords and a Central sweater with three stripes on the sleeve, shuffled out on the stage. He was a stocky fellow, with broad shoulders and powerful arms. The Laurel students gave him a big hand, and he waited awkwardly at the mike until the noise subsided.

"I'm not much of a speaker," he began, grinning, "but I figured I could get out of a couple of classes if I came over here to give this talk, so here I am." The audience laughed. "I'm not sure," he continued, "but maybe I should have stayed in my classes. At least my knees wouldn't be knocking together."

Larry shifted his weight, and tipped the mike Sinatra-fashion.

"Penny said I had a lot of friends here, and I guess she's right. I understand about five hundred of you went to old Central last year. To the old Central gang, I'd like to say *hello!*"

This was greeted by a general outburst of approval.

"About this game tomorrow. We don't think it will be any pushover, because we know that when Coach Hartford turns out a team it is bound to be tough. However, we think we have a good combination at Hilltop. We won our first game against Islandview High last week, and we're going to be out there doing everything possible to make it two in a row. We'll be seeing you."

Larry Bowman left the stage, and the yell team was back before the applause had died away.

Steve Morgan, who was sitting in the back of the audience, left the auditorium and made his way past the boys' locker room in the direction of the stage door. He figured that Larry would be leaving right after his talk, and he was right. He met Larry and Penny coming down the corridor near the custodian's office.

"Hiya, Larry," Steve said, and his voice had in it the friendliness that he really felt toward his former teammate.

"Hello," Larry said, surprised and slightly embarrassed.

Penny walked on a few steps and leaned against a radiator, waiting.

"Just thought I'd say hello before you got away," Steve continued. "Heard you played a swell game against Islandview."

"Thanks. We got a few breaks."

Steve was still wearing his Central High sweater, and these two players should have had much in common, but for some reason there seemed to be a barrier between them. Steve made another effort to carry on the strained conversation.

"Ever see any of the old gang—Big Bill—Skiffo?"

"Yeah. We went skiing last week end. Spent two days up at Mount Baker Lodge."

"That's swell." Steve smiled, but inside he felt the deep stab of Larry's words. They had left him out. The *Rambling Rams* had given him the cold shoulder. "Bet you had a great time," Steve finished weakly.

"Sure did. Well, be seeing you, Steve."

"Yeah. Be seeing you, Larry."

For a moment Steve stood watching Larry and Penny walk down the hall. When they rounded the corner he turned and hurried in the other direction. There was a lump in his throat—a great big lump that would not be denied. He wandered up to the third floor, and for a long time stood in a secluded alcove staring out of the hall window.

It was there that Yogi Zimmerman found him.

"What you doin' up here, Steve?" Yogi asked.

"Thinking," Steve said sharply. "What do you want?"

"I just wanted to give you a picture."

"A picture?"

"Yeah. It's a candid shot of you. I took it in study hall that day I dropped the note."

"Not bad," Steve said, looking at the photograph. "I didn't see you take it."

Yogi unbuttoned his shirt.

"I keep my camera here. I can take pictures of people and they never suspect it. I'm going to be a news photographer."

"Good idea. Thanks for the picture, Yogi, but don't let that camera get you into trouble."

CHAPTER FIVE

STEVE MORGAN was unusually quiet that evening as he took his regular place at the dining-room table. His father, a large, portly man who had played college football while learning the secrets of business administration, peered around the centerpiece at his son, and there was concern in his eyes. His mother darted quick glances at him as she brought the heaping dishes of food from the kitchen, and even his sister, Joan, who was four years older than Steve, and who worked in a downtown office, noticed that Steve was not showing his natural enthusiasm for food.

"What's the matter, Steve?" Joan asked. "Are you sick?"

"No, I'm not sick," Steve snapped.

"Well!" Joan exclaimed, pretending shocked surprise. She edged her chair closer to her father as if looking for protection. "You don't have to bite my head off. I just asked a simple question."

"And I just gave a simple answer," Steve replied.

"Now, children," Mrs. Morgan said, wiping her hands on her apron. She still called Joan and Steve her children, though they were both taller than she. "Now, children, let's not have any bickering, especially at dinner time. Here, Steve, have some of these mashed potatoes. You must eat if you are to keep on the way you do. I'm afraid you're overworking yourself, what with classwork, and football, and all. You don't get enough rest at night. It was after eleven last night, Steve. What would Coach Hartford say?"

"Aw, Mother," Steve mumbled, "quit worrying. I'm not ten years old, you know."

"Your mother is right," Mr. Morgan said. "You aren't getting enough sleep. Now when I was in college . . ."

"But listen, Dad, I get all . . ."

"Steve." Mrs. Morgan spoke severely. "Don't interrupt your father."

"When I was in college," Mr. Morgan continued, "our coach used to go around to the fraternity houses every night and call the roll. Anybody who wanted to play football on his team was in bed by ten."

"Coaches don't do that any more," Steve said. "Times have changed, Dad. In your day a coach was lucky if he could keep eleven men eligible throughout the season.

He had to nurse them along. Now there are more play-ers than a coach knows what to do with. If one fellow can't make the grade there are ten men to take his place."

"Humph!" Mr. Morgan snorted. "Times haven't changed as much as you think. There may be more boys trying to make the team, but for the ones who really count, the rules are pretty much the same as they were in my day. Good food, regular hours for rest, clean liv-ing—those things are rather fundamental."

"But football is streamlined today," Steve said. "The game is wide open."

"I agree with you that football has changed," Mr. Morgan said, "and there is no question about its being a more interesting game now than it was twenty years ago. But the point I want to make is that it takes more skill to play a wide open game. If a player is to be suc-cessful he has to train more carefully than ever before."

"Steve trains, Dad," Joan said, rising to the defense of her brother. "There's such a thing as over-training. It puts a player on edge, makes him irritable."

Steve looked at his sister with new interest.

"Not bad, Sis," he said. "Maybe you've diagnosed my case. Pass the butter, please."

Mrs. Morgan beamed. This was more like Steve. He

was generally calm and unperturbed. She hated to see any change in his manner.

But when the meal was finished, and Joan was helping her mother with the dishes, Steve paced around the living room like a restless lion. He played a couple of new records on the console. This did not seem to quiet him. His father, who was enjoying a cigar in his favorite chair, finally put the evening paper down.

"Haven't you any home work, Steve?" he asked.

Steve shook his head.

"Why don't you sit down and tell me what's really bothering you."

Much to his surprise Steve sprawled out on the davenport and started to talk.

"I saw Larry Bowman today. He was at Laurel giving a talk about the Hilltop game. After the assembly I went out in the hall to talk with him, and he gave me an icy reception. It was as smooth a brush-off as I've ever had."

"What was the reason?"

"I'm not sure, but I imagine it had something to do with the All-city trophy. He said that he and Skiffo Drake and Big Bill Toner went skiing up at Mount Baker."

"What's unusual about that? There are crowds going skiing every week end."

"But don't you see, Dad? They left me out. I was the only one of the old Central backfield that wasn't invited to go. Those fellows all go to different schools now, but they're still friends. If they had wanted me along they would have asked me, but they don't have any time for me now."

"Don't you suppose it is because you elected to go to Laurel High? You know yourself that there has always been strong feeling between old Central pupils and those who attend Laurel."

"Yeah, but they don't have to carry it so far. I'm still willing to be friends with them. In fact, I would rather have it that way. We were all pals at old Central. Just because the school board breaks up the school and I decide to go to Laurel shouldn't be cause for breaking up friendships as well. There's more to it than just attending Laurel High. They're building up some kind of a case against me."

"If it has to do with the All-city trophy, time will clear it up. You know that you didn't take the cup. Your conscience is clear."

"Yeah, but Dad, if they suspect me, and if they talk about me as if I were guilty, look at the reputation I'll get. As a matter of fact, I guess I have the reputation already."

"It's unfortunate, Steve, but there's only one thing to do."

"What's that?"

"Wait. Carry on the best way you know how, and wait. Sooner or later your name will be cleared so far as the trophy is concerned."

"But if they never find the trophy everybody will believe that I took it."

"Only those who like to believe such things will believe it," Mr. Morgan pointed out. "All the others will judge you on your merits."

"But sometimes people misjudge you when you're doing what seems to be the right thing to do," Steve persisted.

"What do you mean?"

"I made a lot of enemies when I sounded off about the student strike at old Central. Perhaps, if I hadn't stuck my neck out . . ."

"There are a lot of people in this world who are afraid to voice their convictions, Steve. If you have thought a matter through and have arrived at what seems to be a sound conviction, then stand up for it, and fight for it, if necessary. It's easy to run away from an issue—to refuse to face it. People will respect you more if you battle it out, even though you may have overwhelming odds against you."

Steve's father picked up the paper again, and Steve stretched out on the davenport and gazed at the ceiling. He was thinking about the things his father had said. He had a feeling that his father was right. At least his words gave him a new slant on the problem, made him feel that perhaps things would eventually work out all right.

Before going to bed that night, Steve spent some time poring over the pictures in the Central annual that had been published the previous June. This was the last annual that would ever be printed at old Central. The pictures brought back pleasant memories of the events that had happened before the announcement that old Central would be closed.

There was a full-page picture of the football team, with the line crouched down, and the backfield standing behind with their hands on their hips. The *Rambling Rams!* There was Skiffo Drake, a lock of hair hanging down over his eyes, and his large nose looking extra large in the bright sunshine. Stocky Larry Bowman stood next to Skiffo. His mouth was twisted in a half smile, and he was squinting at the camera. Next to him, Big Bill Toner looked like some towering lumberjack, with his broad shoulders, his close-cropped hair, and his swarthy skin. Steve looked at his own picture critically. He was not as tall as Big Bill and Skiffo Drake, but he was bigger than Larry Bowman. His features were clean-cut, almost collegiate, and he was the only one of the four who had his hair combed. Steve thought he looked something like his father, only his father had taken on weight in recent years. There was a resemblance to pictures of his father taken in college days when he had been All-coast tackle. There was the same high forehead, the same sharp chin, the same dark eyes. The pads under his jersey only accentuated his square shoulders. They were good, stout shoulders, made for plowing through a tough line.

Coach Hartford, standing with his players, looked just the same as he always looked in his baggy sweatshirt. He had a kid-like grin that was disarming, and he looked young for a coach. If he had been in uniform he might easily have been mistaken for one of the players.

The old Central *Rams!* That team had been a good team. They had lost only one game during the season, and most of the players were juniors. Hilltop High had taken the championship with a heavy, experienced team, but they were washed up. Most of their star players had graduated. This was the year for old Central. This was the year the *Rambling Rams* were going to win the pennant. And now—there was no old Central. The *Rambling Rams* did not exist. Funny how a school could just fold up and disappear in such a short time. True, the building was still standing, but the school was gone. Old Central was dead.

As he turned the pages Steve came to a picture in the feature section that had been taken at the Ski Bowl. Again it was the old Central backfield, but this time it was a silly picture. They were lined up in "T" formation, and they were on skis. The camera had caught them coming down the slope, like a flying backfield. Steve carried a football, and Skiffo, Larry, and Big Bill formed interference. It had been fun taking the picture, but looking at it now made Steve realize more than ever that there was a wide breach between himself and his former friends.

Another picture, taken at a house party across the Sound, showed Steve and Penny Carson sitting on a driftwood log feeding each other large pieces of chocolate cream pie. Steve looked at the picture wistfully. He realized that the house party was the last date he had had with Penny. Well, that was that. There had been no occasion to speak to Penny since, and she had shown no inclination to start a conversation. There were lots of girls at Laurel, but somehow Steve had suddenly lost interest in everything but football.

That night Steve went to his room at ten o'clock. Evidently his father's little lecture had made an impression on him. Perhaps he did need more rest. He undressed slowly and donned his pajamas. Then he stepped into his slippers and a lounging robe and for some time stood in front of the darkened window of his room, gazing out over the city.

Steve's home was on a steep slope overlooking Lake Portage. On the opposite hill he could make out the dark hulk of Hilltop High, silhouetted against a dim sky. Beyond he could see the gold of moonlight on the waters of Puget Sound. The lights of the city spread around the harbor like a sparkling horseshoe, and off in the distance they faded in a soft glow.

Portside was a beautiful city, hemmed in by mountains and lakes and the far reaches of the Sound. Steve thought there was no better place to live in all the world. He knew that he was fortunate to have a good home and a family that cared for the things for which a family stood. His father was hard working and successful. His mother was kind and patient. His sister was good-looking and full of fun most of the time. His older brother, who was married, lived on the lake shore and had a cabin cruiser. Life had been good to Steve Morgan, and until the closing of old Central it had been carefree and happy.

"If they could only have waited until we graduated," Steve said, under his breath.

But old Central was closed. There was little he could do about it. It had marred the pleasant routine of his life, and it had brought problems he had not anticipated. Perhaps his father was right. If he waited long enough, time would clear up his difficulties.

He sank down on the bed and closed his eyes. There was nothing to do but wait.

LAUREL HIGH vs. HILLTOP HIGH

THE LINE-UP

Art Dressel	REL	Don Erickson
Bud Radcliffe	RTL	Jim Eaton
Jack DeCourcey	RGL	Mel Hostmark
Leon Berry	C	Pete Crowder
Syd Johnson	LGR	Shorty Mahill
Will Lanfield	LTR	Rod Whitson
Jim Pearson	LER	Slim Pellet
Lou Shafer	Q	Larry Bowman
Steve Morgan	LHR	Ozz Oscowitz
Ben Eskenazi	F	Johnnie Mercer
Phil MacLain	RHL	Ron Smith

FRIDAY CAME with a burst of sunshine. Steve fidgeted through his morning classes, and at 1:10 he made his way to the athletic locker room. The game with Hilltop started at three, but it was a long way to the Civic Field, and Coach Hartford wanted his team dressed and at the field in plenty of time for the warmup.

Steve sat on the bench in front of his locker and gazed at a little sign one of the managers had plastered to the door with pieces of adhesive tape. It said:

ARE YOU GOING TO LET HILLTOP
STOP YOU?

Steve looked around. Other signs were stuck on other locker doors. Syd Johnson's locker was near by. It had a note that said:

WHO'S GOING TO PUSH WHO AROUND
THIS AFTERNOON?

Psychology! Steve had seen this trick employed before. Somehow it left him cold. What did it matter who pushed who around? This was just a game. Somebody had to win. Somebody had to lose. Ten years from now no one would remember the score.

Steve sat in the back of the bus that took them to the field. He was quiet—almost glum. Art Dressel, lanky right end who sat next to him, was a bundle of nerves. He kept pulling at his sock, twitching his shoulder pads, slapping his knee.

"Going to have a dry field," Art said. "That's a break."

Steve did not reply.

"What's eating you, Morgan?" Art asked. "You look as though you'd lost your last friend."

"Maybe I have," Steve mumbled.

"Aw, cheer up. Life can't be that sad."

Steve tried to grin, but the result was anything but heartwarming.

"Hey, fellows . . . look!" Art grinned, pointing a thumb at Steve. "Frankenstein!"

The game started promptly at three. The stands were full. The bands were playing. The yell leaders were doing handsprings. The coaches were pacing back and forth. The substitutes were standing nervously in front of their benches. The referee signaled the captains. The

whistle blew, and Laurel kicked off to the Hilltop *Cougars.*

The ball floated high in the air, twisting lazily to fall with a thump into the arms of Larry Bowman on the ten-yard line. Larry ran it back to the twenty, the twenty-five, the thirty, where Art Dressel wrapped his

long arms around Larry's legs, and the Hilltop quarterback was down.

Hilltop came out of the huddle with determined
steps. Larry Bowman had called a play off center, but
it piled up at the scrimmage line. When the players un-
tangled themselves, Syd Johnson was at the bottom of

the pile. Steve smiled to himself. Evidently Syd Johnson had taken the locker room note seriously. Syd was not going to be pushed around by Hilltop this afternoon.

Hilltop tried one more running play, and then a short pass that failed. They kicked on the third down. The game was young, and they were playing it safe.

Steve took the kick on his own twenty and ran it back to the midfield stripe before he was stopped.

As he walked to the huddle he was dimly conscious of a cheer that came drifting from the Laurel stands.

Morgan——Rah! Rah! Rah!——Morgan!

A strange feeling swept over him. They were calling his name, those hundreds of pupils in the Laurel rooting section. Suddenly, all of the tension of the past few days was gone. For awhile he forgot that he was one of the Phantom Backfield men from old Central. He felt at ease, and a new strength seemed to surge through his body. In the huddle Art Dressel had his arm around Steve's shoulder.

"How you doin', Frankenstein?" Art asked.

"Okay," Steve answered, grinning.

Lou Shafer was talking. "Number twelve. Got it?"

Number twelve was a wide end run, with Phil Mac-Lain packing the ball. Steve and Eskenazi ran interference. The play pulled Johnson out of the line to help clear the way. If Pearson boxed the Hilltop end, it was a power play, good for the secondary, and with a little down-field blocking it could go places.

When the referee's whistle sounded, Phil MacLain was sprawled on the Hilltop thirty-five, and it was first down for Laurel.

"Now we're loggin'," Shafer said, as they huddled for the next play. "Number eight. Got it?"

Eight was a short pass, and it clicked.

Second down, two to go.

Eskenazi punched it over for another first down, and the ball was on Hilltop's twenty-one-yard line.

"Lay off the left side of their line," Eskenazi said in the huddle. "Eaton and Erickson are dynamite. Keep hitting the right side." It was good advice.

Play by play, yard by yard, they worked the ball toward the goal, and the quarter was only ten minutes old when Eskenazi scored with a line plunge from the five-yard marker.

The Laurel stands went wild. It was their first touchdown of the season, and it had come so smoothly that it heralded other scores in the future.

Phil MacLain kicked the try-for-point, and the scoreboard read: LAUREL 7, HILLTOP 0.

As Steve walked back to his position for the next

kickoff he tried to account for the feeling that had come over him. This was not his school, and yet, when they had put that touchdown over, he had experienced a faint tingle of elation. It was not as strong as in the old days at Central High, but it was there, nevertheless.

But if there was elation with that first touchdown, there were some anxious moments ahead. In the second quarter the Hilltop defense stiffened, and at the same time their offense started to roll. A long pass put them deep in Laurel territory, and when they had worked it down to the fifteen, Larry Bowman shook himself loose on a quarterback sneak and scampered across for a Hilltop score. They missed the try-for-point, but the touchdown gave them confidence, and before the half was over the *Cougars* had hammered their way through for another touchdown, and the scoreboard read: HILL-TOP 12, LAUREL 7.

Coach Hartford talked to the Laurel team during the half.

"You looked good on that first touchdown. Do you know what did it for you? Blocking. Get a man off his feet and he's out of the play. That's blocking. What good is a backfield without a line? Only one man can carry the ball. What do you other ten men do? You block. If you aren't packing the ball you're supposed to be helping the ball carrier. How? By blocking. If you just want to watch the game, you might as well go up in the stands. You can see it better from there. If you want to play the game, well, get in there and block. You hear me? *Block!*"

Hartford waited for the idea to soak in. Then he started with Dressel, right end.

"Did you hear me, Dressel? What are you supposed to do?"

"Block," Dressel said.

"Did you hear me, Radcliffe? What are you supposed to do?"

"Block," Radcliffe said.

By the time he got around to Phil MacLain he had made his point clear.

The pay-off? It came in the first minute of the second half.

Hilltop kicked off to Laurel and Eskenazi brought it back to the thirty. MacLain gained six off the right side. Then Steve Morgan's number was up.

Steve took the ball on a pass from Shafer. He started around end, saw a hole, cut in. He was through without a hand touching him, but the Hilltop secondary was converging on him, so he switched to the right. Only two players were able to switch with him. Steve figured he could make the fifty-yard line before they got him. He saw a dark form coming up on his left. It was Lanfield, left tackle for Laurel. Lanfield took one man out with a perfect block.

Then Leon Berry, Laurel center, appeared from no-where and rolled into the other Hilltop player. They went down in a heap, and Steve skirted their kicking feet. The path was wide open.

Steve turned on the steam. His powerful legs drove ahead, his cleats dug into the turf. He was a flashing whirlwind, swishing along the sideline. There was no one between him and the goal line.

But three other Hilltop players had recovered from their first drive and were cutting across the field toward him. They had a shorter distance to run. They could intercept him. Steve could not see Syd Johnson coming down the field a few steps behind him. Syd was heading for the first of those Hilltop players, and he mowed him down.

Lou Shafer took the second man out, and then it was a race between Steve and the third Hilltop player. Steve won. He cut the goal line in the corner, and loped around in the end zone. After the try-for-point the score read: LAUREL 14, HILLTOP 12.

This time the Laurel section was a madhouse.

Morgan——Rah! Rah! Rah!——Morgan!

But Steve knew that yell was not for him alone. As the Laurel team gathered in the huddle before the next kickoff, Steve was still puffing, but he managed to grin at his teammates.

"Thanks, gang," he said. "That was blocking."

It was not until the fourth quarter was well along that Steve thought of Yogi Zimmerman. The little freshman had predicted that Laurel would win 21 to 12. It would be too bad to disappoint Yogi. There were five minutes left to play. Laurel had the ball on the Hilltop forty-eight. It was third down, six to go.

In the huddle Lou Shafer looked at Steve.

"Number twenty-four," he said.

That was a long pass, with both ends and a halfback down to receive. Steve was the halfback, and he knew why Lou was looking at him. He nodded.

They came out of the huddle. Steve moved to his position to the left, and the Hilltop line shifted. Eskenazi took the ball, dropped back to pass. He had good protection, but one end threatened and he ran to the left.

Steve had streaked straight down the sideline. When he reached the thirty-yard marker he cut to the right, and ran on a slant toward the opposite corner of the field. The ends had pulled the secondary wide open.

Steve was alone, with one man coming up. When he reached the ten-yard line he turned quickly and there, right over his shoulder, like a transport plane coming in to land, was the pigskin. Steve wrapped his hands around the spiraling oval, and without breaking his stride raced across for the final score.

The try-for-point was good, and Lou Shafer slapped Steve on the shoulder.

"It's queer," he said, rubbing his chin. "Twenty-one to twelve. That's the score you predicted in the shower room last Monday."

"It's strange, all right," Steve said, "but I didn't predict the score. I just repeated what a little freshman told me."

"A freshman?"

"Yeah. Funny little guy, with red hair and a million freckles. His name is Yogi. Yogi Zimmerman."

*There . . . like a transport plane coming in to land, was
the pigskin*

CHAPTER SEVEN

Yogi's real name was Carl, but only his teachers and his parents called him by that name. To everyone else he was just Yogi. The nickname had followed him through grade school, and now high school. Carl had accepted the name as a tribute from his classmates. He was always fooling them with tricks, and when he completely baffled them there was general agreement that Carl Zimmerman was possessed of some magical powers. Only Carl knew that this was not so, but if they wanted to call him Yogi he had no objection. It was something like the word "doctor" applied to one who possessed healing powers. It was a mark of distinction.

Yogi was not one to look down upon distinction. In fact, that was one of the things he desired most. For distinction meant recognition, and Yogi was the type of boy who could never win recognition unless he developed some trait that would set him apart from his fellowmen. He was the kind of boy who got lost in crowds. Nobody paid much attention to him. When leaders in the school gathered in a huddle during the noon hour Yogi was one of the boys on the fringe of the group. Seldom was he accepted in the inner circle.

This was partly due to his size, and partly to the fact that along some lines he had not reached the level of maturity that other boys expected of him. To compensate for his lack of athletic ability, Yogi had made a study of sport records that went far back into the past. He had an encyclopedic mind in this respect. He could tell you what team won the World Series in 1908, or who was chosen for the quarterback position on Walter Camp's All-American team in 1911, or he could go into detail on the feat of Bobby Jones in 1930, when he set an all-time record in winning the four major golf championships in one season.

Only in one sport did Yogi excel. That was skiing. Yogi's father was an expert skier, and when Yogi was four years old his father had bought him his first pair of skis. Yogi took naturally to the sport, and when he was seven or eight he was skimming down the steepest courses with the confidence of an expert. His father taught him all of the tricks—the snow-plow, the stem turn, the christie. The Zimmermans had a cabin at Snoqualmie Pass, and every week end when the weather was right Yogi and his father could be found enjoying the mountain slopes, and the thrill of a down-hill race with the wind whipping and powder snow flying from their waxed boards.

Another interest that consumed much of Yogi's spare time was to be found on the shelves of the neighborhood lending library. Yogi was a detective-story fan. Ellery Queen and Dashiell Hammett were among his favorite authors, though he welcomed lesser-known writers and admired them greatly if they could keep him in suspense until the end. Many a night Yogi had taken the works of such authors to bed with him, and long after the official time for "lights-out" in the Zimmerman household, he had kept his flashlight burning under the covers to finish an exciting book.

There were times when Yogi dreamed of being a great detective—a smooth operator like The Thin Man. In his imagination, the police stood in awe of his great deductive powers, and gangsters fled in alarm when Yogi Zimmerman was called in to clear up some puzzling mystery. His dreams always ended with the reward of glaring headlines and public acclaim. At the age of ten he had his own fingerprinting outfit, and he started a card-filing system that carried complete identification on every youngster within a radius of ten blocks. Yogi might have grown up to become the world' greatest detective had not a wealthy aunt given him a fine camera for his eleventh birthday. That camera changed the whole course of Yogi Zimmerman's interesting life.

Yogi plunged into the field of photography like a toad diving into a pool. All of the profits from his paper route went into the purchase of film and developing equipment. He cleared out a basement room back of the furnace and turned it into a laboratory. It was ideal for a darkroom, and it was there that he developed his own pictures. At the age of twelve he had given up all thought of becoming a detective and had but one aim in life—to become the world's greatest news photographer. That he was serious about this new venture was evidenced by his savings account. He had more than one hundred dollars in the bank. As soon as the sum reached two hundred he knew where he could purchase a slightly used Speed Graphic with synchronized flash equipment—the kind of camera used by news photographers. At the age of thirteen he owned the new camera, and Yogi Zimmerman was well on his way toward his newly discovered profession.

Yogi's ability to predict football scores might have seemed remarkable to anyone but Yogi. He took it as a matter of course. The Hilltop game was not the first game that he had called with uncanny accuracy.

Yogi was waiting at the sidelines to congratulate Steve when the team came off the field.

Steve put his arm around the freshman. "How did you know what the score would be?"

"I didn't," Yogi said innocently. "I just guessed, that's all."

Steve rumpled Yogi's hair.

"You better polish up your crystal ball, then. We play Wallingford High next."

CHAPTER EIGHT

In spite of a "charley horse" that tugged persistently at the muscles of his thigh, Steve Morgan felt good on the ride back from the Civic Field to Laurel High. The crimson-and-silver team had won a game. The Laurel *Hawks* had soared over the heads of the Hilltop players, and Larry Bowman's eleven had tasted its first defeat of the season by the score of 21 to 12.

Funny, Steve thought, as the bus rumbled over the city streets, that Yogi Zimmerman should have called the turn so accurately. It was luck, of course, that he had predicted the exact score, but he had done more than that. He had credited Steve Morgan with two touchdowns long before the game was played, and that was the way it had worked out. The more Steve thought about Yogi, the more puzzled he became.

The odor of leather and sweat and rubbing alcohol pervaded the bus, but nobody seemed to mind. The team was happy. Wisecracks were on everyone's tongue, and there was much laughter.

As the bus rounded the corner near the school and the imposing brick front of Laurel High came into view, Steve had a peculiar feeling that he could not explain. A little tingle went down his spine, and the muscles of his throat tightened. Only a moment, and it was gone. Queer—that feeling! He had known it before in the old days at Central High, but that he could explain. There was deep love in his heart for the ivy-covered walls of the old building. They stood for warmth and friendship, for scholarship and athletic pride. They were different from the walls of Laurel High—three stories of red brick with white granite cornices, and row upon row of shimmering windows that gave the building the appearance of some modern air-conditioned factory. For what did these walls stand? Could it be that they stood for the same things that were to be found within the walls of old Central? No. Steve brushed the thought from his mind. These walls could never stand for all the traditions that were packed into the years of old Central. And yet, there was that fleeting tingle down his spine. It had stirred from some hidden depth of emotion. When it was gone it left him bothered, confused.

Laurel drew a bye in the city schedule for the following week. Even Coach Hartford welcomed the rest, for he had been working under pressure. He had been striving to build a team out of eleven players, and the victory over Hilltop was the first faint glimmer of success. Now if he could bring this team along, keep the players in the right psychological frame of mind, smooth out the weak spots, there was a chance, an outside chance . . .

Hartford held a light drill on Monday, just enough to get the kinks out of tired muscles. Tuesday they worked on plays, polishing one formation, correcting the timing on another. A half-hour scrimmage sent them to the showers feeling like frisky colts being rounded into a corral. Wednesday the first team was lined up against the second team. For the past three days Hartford's assistant had been drilling this second team on some of the Wallingford plays.

"Wallingford is next on our schedule," Coach Hartford said. "This won't be any set-up. Wallingford has won two in a row. They beat Airport High 34 to 6, and that means they pack a lot of power. They took Ravenna 12 to 0. Figure it out for yourselves. You played Ravenna. By comparative scores Wallingford has a better team than Laurel. They have Big Bill Toner playing full. Big Bill is a regular piledriver. If you can stop Big Bill you might skin through this one. If you can't stop him it will be curtains."

Steve Morgan knew that Coach Hartford was right. Big Bill Toner had been the powerhouse for the *Rambling Rams* at old Central. Big Bill was the man to watch.

A 200-pound sophomore named Bond was playing Big Bill's position on the Laurel second team, and for the next hour Bond took a beating that was more than he had bargained for. Every time he packed the ball it seemed as if the entire first team pounced on him, and when the scrimmage was over Bond staggered to his feet, battered and bruised.

"Never again," Bond muttered, as he trudged to the showers. "Big Bill Toner can have that job, and he's welcome to it."

On Friday Wallingford High played Forest High. Coach Hartford canceled practice for that day, and instructed his entire Laurel team to attend the game.

"Keep your eye on Big Bill Toner," the coach said. "You're going to play this game in the stands. Every time Big Bill gets the ball I want you to figure out just how you would get him if you were down on the field."

Friday was an ideal day for football, and Steve welcomed an early dismissal and the chance to sit in the stands and watch a game. He missed the bus that took most of the players to the game, so he had to ride alone on the trolley. He arrived at the Civic Field just as the two teams were lining up for the kickoff. The stands were crowded, and he was unable to find the other Laurel players. He took a seat high in the south stands and settled down with a box of popcorn, a smile of anticipation on his face. He was surrounded by Forest High students, and there was nobody near him whom he knew. That is, he thought he was among strangers, but when he looked more closely at the boy sitting next to him he found himself staring into the grinning face of Yogi Zimmerman.

"Hiya, Steve," Yogi said, squinting his eyes so that the round freckles on his cheeks stretched into little football shapes. "Nice day for a game."

"Yogi," Steve said. "What are you doing here? Haven't you a sixth period class?"

"Not today."

"Skipping?"

"Don't be silly. I'm A.W.O.L."

"What's the difference?"

"Much more dignified."

Steve offered the freshman some popcorn, and Yogi took a generous handful which he managed to dispose of in one mouthful.

"Who's going to win today?" Steve asked.

"Wall'n'ford," Yogi mumbled through the pop-corn.

"What makes you so sure?"

"It's in the bag."

When the gun sounded, ending the first half, it looked as if Yogi were right again. The Wallingford *Ducks* led by a score of 21 to 7. Two of the touchdowns had been made by Big Bill Toner, who had powered his way through the Forest line for long gains.

During the halftime intermission most of the Forest pupils drifted down for hot dogs and pop, but Steve and Yogi Zimmerman sat tight. They were working on their third box of popcorn when five fellows converged on them from the aisle. They were hatless. One wore a red plaid stag shirt, three wore navy surplus jackets, and the fourth wore a tan topcoat. They looked like seniors, and they sat down on both sides of Steve and Yogi, but they paid little attention to the freshman.

"You Steve Morgan?" one of them asked, keeping his tone down so that others would not hear.

Steve nodded.

"We're from Mercer High," one of them said. "We want to get something straight."

"Okay," Steve said. "What?"

"We happen to know you swiped the All-city silver cup from the trophy case at old Central. Where is it?"

"You guys are off the beam," Steve replied.

"You were in the building the night the cup disappeared."

Steve nodded.

"Everybody from old Central knows you got it."

"That's where you're wrong," Steve said. "If you fellows are from Mercer High how does it happen you're so interested in the All-city cup? It was a Central High trophy."

"We've been accused of stealin' it."

" 'We?' " There was a question in Steve's voice.

"The Owls. Our chapter at Mercer High was hauled on the carpet."

" 'The Owls?' " Steve repeated, pretending ignorance.

"Don't play dumb," one of the fellows answered. "You know the Owls have a chapter in every high school in Portside. Well, our members don't like being accused of stealin' that mug. It puts us in a bad light, see."

"Sure. I can see that. If you didn't steal the cup, and if you are accused of stealing it, that looks bad. Anything could happen. You might be expelled. Your club might be suspended."

"That's the rough idea. Now when are you going to produce the cup and clear our record?"

"I'm afraid that's impossible," Steve protested. "As I said before, I don't have the cup."

"An' we don't believe you." It was the fellow in the stag shirt who was talking now. "Listen, Morgan, we're giving you one week to kick through with the All-city cup."

"And if I *don't* produce it?"

"That's your hard luck."

With this vague threat hanging in the air, the five fellows departed as abruptly as they had come, leaving Steve with a queer feeling in the pit of his stomach, and Yogi Zimmerman with a mouthful of popcorn that he had forgotten to chew.

"Why, those big lugs . . ." Yogi said, jumping up belligerently, but Steve quickly shoved him back in his seat.

"Finish your popcorn," Steve said.

"But those guys threatened you!"

"Sure. They're on the spot. They'll cool off. Give them time."

In the second half Big Bill Toner scored one more touchdown for Wallingford, but they missed the try-for-point. When the game ended the scoreboard showed 27 to 7 in favor of the *Ducks*.

As the crowd filed out of the stands, Yogi tagged along with Steve Morgan. They had to wait at the corner for a trolley, and Yogi leaned against a telephone pole, deep in thought.

"What's bothering you?" Steve asked, half amused at Yogi's solemn concentration.

"I'm just thinking," Yogi said.

"Trying to figure out how the Wallingford-Laurel game will come out?"

"Nope. I got that figured out. We're going to win, but it will be close. Heads-up football will do it, but we can't do it if we start playing blindman's buff. Nope. I was thinking about something more important than a football game. I was thinking about a missing football trophy."

"Don't tell me you know where it is."

Yogi Zimmerman shook his head. "I don't know where it is. But I'm worried, Steve. If they're going to hang this job on you, maybe I'd better go to work on it. First, though, you have to tell me the whole story."

On the way home Steve told Yogi Zimmerman all that he knew about the missing trophy.

"How'd the story get around that you were in the building the night the cup disappeared?" Yogi asked.

Steve shook his head. "Pretty hard to trace a rumor."

"But a rumor has to start somewhere. What was that club the Mercer gang belonged to?"

"The Owls."

"What kind of an outfit is that?"

"Social club," Steve said. "They give dances and parties. Several of them started up after the school board outlawed fraternities. They hold meetings in their homes."

"Did you know any of the Owls at old Central?"

"I knew two or three members," Steve said. "They didn't rate much."

"Hmmmm!" Yogi Zimmerman sat in silence for some time. When the trolley reached his corner he slapped Steve on the shoulder.

"Be seein' you," the freshman said. "If I get an idea I'll give you a ring."

CHAPTER NINE

YOGI CALLED Steve Morgan the following morning, but it was not because he had an idea about the missing trophy. He had plans for a ski trip.

"Dad and I are going up to the cabin for the week end," Yogi said. "How would you like to go along?"

"Nothing I'd like better," Steve said, "but I won't be able to do much skiing. Hartford has declared a ban on skiing during the football season. He's afraid of injuries."

"Why not go along for the trip?" Yogi suggested. "I'd like to have Dad get acquainted with you."

"I'm a pretty good cook," Steve said, "and I'm a demon at washing dishes."

"You're hired," Yogi enthused. "Good dish washers are hard to find."

"What time are you leaving?" Steve asked.

"About noon."

"Okay. I'll take my skis along for the sake of appearance. I can spend the week end waxing them."

At noon Mr. Zimmerman drove up in front of Steve's house. He had a new car with long sleek lines and a two-tone paint job.

"Whew!" Steve exclaimed under his breath as Yogi hopped out and ran up the front steps.

Steve opened the door.

"All set?" Yogi said. "We're right on the nose."

"So I notice," Steve replied. He slipped into his ski jacket and gathered up his skis and poles.

"Dad, this is Steve Morgan," Yogi said, pride in his voice.

"I'm glad to know you, Steve," Mr. Zimmerman said. "Carl tells me you're quite a football player."

"Who? Oh, you mean Yogi," Steve said, laughing. "I'm not used to hearing him called Carl."

"Here, let me help you." Mr. Zimmerman fitted Steve's skis in the rack that was mounted on top of the car. "We can all ride in the front seat. There's plenty of room."

Steve waved to his mother as the car pulled away from the curb.

"This is a pretty fine car," Steve enthused.

"We were fortunate to get it," Yogi's father said. "Our old car was about ready to fall apart. I guess the dealer took pity on us."

They drove through the city, and crossed the Lake Bridge that led to the cross-state highway.

"We ought to have good skiing," Yogi said. "According to the paper there's fresh snow in the mountains."

"Too bad you can't ski, Steve," Mr. Zimmerman said, "but your coach is right. A football player should stay off skis during the playing season."

"I'll get plenty of it this winter," Steve said. "Last Christmas I spent most of the holidays up in the hills."

"We're lucky in Portside," Mr. Zimmerman said. "We seldom have snow in the city, but in less than two hours we can drive to the finest skiing areas in the world."

"You're right," Steve said. "I remember last year we went skiing at Mount Rainier and swimming in Puget Sound on the same day."

The car was skimming along the shore of Lake Sammamish, and they dipped down over the flats near Issaquah. After a few miles they were starting the long gradual climb that would take them into the foothills of the Cascades, and up the west side of the mountains to Snoqualmie Pass.

Steve settled back in the soft cushions and watched the forest-green hills slip past. It was fun to be rolling along this broad highway, heading for a week end that would be quite different from the routine of football practice.

"How do you like thick, juicy steaks," Yogi asked, "smothered in onions?"

"That language I can understand." Steve grinned.

"That's what we're having for dinner tonight. Three luscious T-bones."

"The trip is a success," Steve drooled. "I can taste them already."

"Just thought I'd mention it," Yogi said, with a sly twinkle in his eye. "It'll give you something to look forward to as long as you can't ski."

They ran into snow above North Bend, and Mr. Zimmerman pulled into a gas station where they put chains on the rear wheels. The rest of the trip was made cautiously. When they finally reached the cabin, which was a short distance from the ski area, they found snow five feet deep on each side of the highway. Snow plows had cleared a parking space, and they had to hike a quarter of a mile from the car. They took food and sleeping bags in on their first trip, and then Yogi and Steve returned for the skis.

When they reached the cabin on the second trip,

Yogi's father had already kindled a blaze in the large stone fireplace. Steve looked around the room in admiration.

The main living room was large, with a bearskin rug in the center and peeled log furniture that gave just the rustic touch needed in such a lodge. Snowshoes were crossed above the mantle, and framed photographs of winter scenes adorned the walls. A kitchen with a huge wood range was at the rear of the cabin, and there were sleeping rooms with built-in bunks off the balcony. Hand-hewn timbers supported the steep roof, and the interior was sealed with knotty pine boards.

"Make yourself at home," Yogi said. "You'll find all the modern conveniences except inside plumbing and electric lights."

"This is great," Steve said, removing his jacket and backing up to the warm fire. "I've been skiing up here a hundred times and I didn't realize there were cabins like this."

"It's Forest Service land," Mr. Zimmerman explained. "We lease it from the government, but we have to build our own cabins. If we ever decide to give it up we just sell the cabin and the new owner takes over the lease."

"Good idea," Steve commented. "How many cabins are there in this area?"

"About fifty. We built this lodge ten years ago, and we've never wanted to give it up."

"I don't blame you. It's perfect."

After a quick lunch, Yogi and his father started waxing their skis. Steve moved to the large leaded-glass window and looked out on a white wonderland. The cabin was in the tall fir timber of the Snoqualmie National Forest, and the branches of the trees were laden with snow. Large flakes drifted down from the gray sky, adding a new soft blanket to the countless layers that had already fallen.

"Nothing like fresh snow," Mr. Zimmerman said, "to brighten things up. It's like new paint on an old barn."

"It seems hard to realize," Steve said, "that only this morning we were basking in the sunshine down in Portside."

"Nothing like variety," Yogi said, putting the finishing touches on his skis. "How about it, Steve? Are you going over to the hill with us?"

"Sure," Steve replied. "I'll do a little lodge skiing today. I can't break a leg skiing on the verandah."

"Perhaps some of the fellows from school will be over there," Yogi said. "There's always a gang hanging around the lodge."

Steve wore ski pants and boots. He pulled on his

heavy jacket and followed Yogi and his father down the path that led to the highway.

It was a short walk up the road, and then they turned right through a canyon of snow that led to the ski area. Here were headquarters for the ski patrol, as well as a spacious public lodge. The hills were crowded with skiers who had come from the city to spend a day on the white slopes. The ski tows were getting a good work-out, the long cables moving endlessly over the huge pulleys mounted high on the hillside. Skiers gripped the cable at the bottom of the hill and in a few minutes were pulled to the take-off spots near the timberline.

"We'll ski for a couple of hours and then we'll head back for the cabin and start dinner," Mr. Zimmerman said. "Think you can keep busy for that long a time?"

"Don't worry about me," Steve said. "I'll find some of the fellows around the lodge."

Yogi and his father clamped their ski harnesses to their boots, and started toward the foot of the ski tow. Steve made his way in the direction of the lodge. He wished that Coach Hartford had not been so strict on his training rules, for there was nothing he would have liked better than to join Yogi and his dad on the slope, but he realized that the coach had good reasons for drawing the line at skiing.

It was warm in the lodge, and Steve unfastened his

jacket and pulled off his ski mittens. The lunch counter was doing a brisk business as Steve seated himself and ordered a bowl of chili. He recognized a group of Laurel pupils down the counter, and they grinned and shouted "Hi!" Steve nodded and grinned in return. One of the fellows was Hank Bartlett, who sat behind him in chemistry. Steve didn't know the girls in the party, but they smiled and Steve took it for granted they were from Laurel.

When they had finished, Hank Bartlett left the group and came over to Steve.

"Getting in a little skiing on the side?" Hank asked.

Steve shook his head. "Just came along for the ride," he said. "Skiing is out until football is over."

"Sorry you can't join us. We've been on the hill since eight this morning."

"You must have got an early start."

"I'll say. Left before daylight. Lot of the gang up here today. The Laurel ski team is training for the cross-country."

"Good," Steve said. "I'll probably see them when they come in. Guess I'll have to be the reception committee."

"Not much excitement hanging around the lodge." Hank was sympathetic.

"I'll have to pass up the excitement this trip."

"Well, be seeing you."

Hank left with the others in his party, and Steve turned to his bowl of chili with renewed interest. He was pleased that Hank had come over to talk with him. Of course, the fact that they were in the same chemistry class gave them something in common. It was not often that Steve felt that he really belonged to Laurel High, and when incidents like this happened his mind was in an uncertain state. Perhaps he did belong to Laurel High. Perhaps the ties that bound one to a school were simple ties of friendship—nothing more. Steve's mind played around with this idea. The sense of well-being that came from being accepted in a school came from the pupils and the faculty, not the building. A school was just a structure made of brick and steel, of wood and cement. Without a faculty and pupils the school would not exist. The sentiment that one built up for a school, then, was simply the result of pleasant association, of loyalty, of rivalry, and even of gratitude for the opportunity to learn. That last item bothered Steve a little. He knew that young people were not greatly concerned with gratitude. That would come later, when their minds had matured.

For some time Steve had been conscious of a change in his own attitude toward school. As he grew older and observed the ways that people live in this world, he had come to the conclusion that an education was essential to the kind of life he hoped to live. He did not know just when he had come to that conclusion, but he had a feeling that it was the result of his associations at old Central. The change to Laurel High had left him a bit shaken, a bit puzzled, but now he was making new associations and slowly they were leading him to the same conclusion. Perhaps they would add up to sentiment before he was through at Laurel High. There had been a time when he thought such a thing was impossible, but now he was not sure.

A noisy group of boys and girls pushed through the doors to the lodge. They were laughing and joking and shaking snow from their jackets and ski caps. One fellow wore a big "W" on his sweater, and Steve recognized him as Jay Clark, who played left guard for Wallingford High. It was obvious that they wanted attention, and they were getting it.

They stamped their feet as they pushed up to the counter. One fellow produced a comb and ran it through black, wavy hair clear to the nape of his neck where he patted the last curling ends in place. He put the comb in his breast pocket, and then started pounding on the counter.

"Service!" he demanded in a loud tone. "We're starved. How about some service?"

Steve looked up at this new outburst. He was not surprised when he recognized the loud-voiced skier. He was Blink Kennedy.

The last time Steve had seen Blink Kennedy was when Blink had objected to his talk in the Beanery after the announcement that old Central was to be closed. That seemed long ago to Steve, and he had hoped that this character would never march through another chapter of his life. But here he was, as arrogant as ever. Steve hunched over his food, hoping that he would not be recognized.

"Two hamburgers and a cup of java," Blink boomed, still pounding the counter for emphasis.

The girl behind the counter, who had ignored his first demand, gave him an ice-cold stare.

"Take it easy, Tarzan," she said. "If you want coffee we'll have to have a note from your mother."

"I've been insulted," Blink stormed. "Who's running this lodge? I want to see the manager."

"I'm the manager," the girl said. "What can I do for you?"

Blink should have been squelched by that reply, but he was not the kind who took humiliation gracefully.

He was about to make some smart rejoinder when Jay Clark interfered.

"Lay off, Blink," Jay said. "She'll have the ski patrol on your neck. They'll kick you off the hill."

"Let 'em kick me off the hill," Blink snorted. "I've been kicked off better hills than this."

"Pipe down," Jay said, pulling Blink away. Blink was finally convinced that he was talking out of turn. Jay turned to the girl behind the counter. "You'll have to excuse my loud-mouthed friend," he said, in his most placating tone. "He's always shooting off his face. Gets him in a lot of trouble. If he can have a cup of coffee and a doughnut to dunk, he'll be happy."

One of the other fellows had taken Blink back to a table and had shoved him into a chair. Jay, by means of an ingratiating smile, had won the manager's approval, and she was ready to fill his order.

Steve's mouth twisted in a wry smile. Blink was still running true to form. He had been a thoroughly unlikable fellow at Central High, and this little episode proved that he had not changed much since he had moved to Wallingford High.

Steve finished his chili, but he remained at the counter and ordered a cup of coffee. He took his time drinking it. Blink had not seen him, and so long as Steve's back was turned to the Wallingford group, there was not much chance of his being recognized. Steve's main reason for wanting to avoid Blink was the fear of a scene. There was no telling what Blink might do. Steve had no qualms about his ability to take care of himself in an encounter with Blink, but why aggravate an old sore. Their fight in the Beanery had been a rather indecisive affair, but that was because other pupils had interfered. Steve had crossed off his battle with Blink as an unpleasant incident, and he preferred to let it go at that.

When Steve finished his coffee, the Wallingford crowd was still huddled around its table. Steve decided to go into the lounge and find a good magazine and a comfortable chair. He would spend an hour or two reading. He paid his check, and slid from the stool.

As he started across the room, he was conscious that Blink Kennedy was rising from the table. Blink had recognized him.

"Well, if it isn't the *great* Steve Morgan," Blink said, pushing his chair back and swaggering in Steve's direction.

Steve continued toward the lounge, but Blink intercepted him when he was halfway across the room. He caught Steve by the sleeve.

"Seems we have a little unfinished business to settle," Blink taunted.

"Forget it, Blink," Steve said. "That's all dead and buried."

" 'Dead and buried,' my eye! Trouble with you, Steve Morgan—you're yellow."

Steve looked at Blink through narrowed eyes. When he spoke his words were clipped.

"You're asking for it, Blink. Come on outside."

"Outside, nothing. What's wrong with right here?"

As Blink spoke his fist came swinging in a fast hay-maker. Steve was unprepared for it, and the crashing blow landed close to his eye and sent him staggering back against a table. He lost his balance, and slipped to his knee.

Blink rushed him and landed another chopping blow against the side of Steve's head. The impact of the lunge sent Steve sprawling against the wall, his head hitting the rough boards with a resounding crack. For a minute there were little stars exploding in Steve's head. His mind was fuzzy, but he knew that he had to do something in a hurry. He jumped to his feet, and just avoided getting kneed as Blink rushed him again.

Steve gave Blink a push and followed him, hanging

on. He shook his head, and as the stars died away Steve found his feet again. He felt a surge of power in his arms and legs. He was hampered by his heavy jacket, but at least he had gained a position where he could defend himself.

Blink was lunging at him, arms swinging in an effort to land another blow, but Steve stood his ground, took the blows on his arms, and shoved Blink away. The suddenness of Blink's attack was gone now, and Steve was breathing more freely. He took a deep breath and moved back when Blink rushed him. He could feel strength rising in him as he warded off Blink's wildly flailing arms. This was it. Blink had walked into this with his eyes open, and there was only one thing for Steve to do. Go to work.

He started moving toward Blink cautiously, like a stalking animal. Blink circled around toward the counter, and when Steve found himself within reach he feinted with his left and sent a slashing right into Blink's jaw. Blink's head snapped back but he recovered, got his arms up to protect his face.

That was just what Steve wanted. Like a ramrod, his left smashed into Blink's stomach. Blink grunted and doubled up. He backed away, tried to lift his head, but Steve was there with an uppercut that started down

Steve had plenty of medicine in his two fists

around his knees. There was the crash of bone against bone as Steve's fist collided with Blink's jaw.

From the corner of his eye Steve could see the Wallingford fellows who had come with Blink. He half expected them to join in the fight, but for some reason they held off. The expression on their faces seemed to say, "It's Blink's affair. Let him take his medicine."

Steve had plenty of medicine in his two fists, and he gave Blink a good dose. A right to the head. A left to the chin. Blink was puffing like a walrus, and trying to cover up with his hands.

As he backed away, Steve followed Blink with slashing blows that jabbed and punched and cut at his battered face. Finally Blink's hands dropped to his sides, and at the same instant Steve's fist exploded in his face. Blink sagged to his knees, toppled on one side, and stretched out on the floor like a rag doll. He was out cold.

Steve turned toward the other Wallingford fellows, but not one of them moved toward him.

Steve's eye was swollen shut, but he managed a grin.

"Sorry I had to do that, fellows, but he's your boy now. When he comes around tell him I'll be in the lounge if he wants to finish this business."

CHAPTER TEN

STEVE DID not remain in the lounge. His eye was beginning to feel uncomfortable, and as he gingerly explored it with his finger-tips he decided that it needed some attention.

When he returned to the dining room, Blink Kennedy and his friends had left. Steve made his way to the counter where the waitress greeted him with a big smile.

"You certainly knocked that fellow off his high horse," she said.

"Too bad I had to do it here," Steve apologized. "I tried to get him outside, but he couldn't wait to take a poke at me."

"He had it coming. What are you going to do about that eye?"

"I don't know. How would beefsteak work on it?"

"I've heard it helps."

"Maybe I could buy a piece of raw steak from you. I'll take it down to the cabin and fix my eye."

The girl cut a generous piece of raw beef for Steve.

"How much do I owe you?" Steve asked.

"Not a thing. You have it coming for finishing off that pest."

"Thanks." Steve grinned.

He made his way back to the Zimmerman cabin, and after he had thrown some wood on the fire, he found adhesive tape and gauze in the first-aid kit. He plastered the beef over his sore eye.

At five o'clock Yogi and his father came in.

"Don't get alarmed at my appearance," Steve said with a smile. "I collided with a haymaker."

"We heard about it," Yogi said. "Must have been quite a fight. The whole lodge is talking about it."

"Let's see that eye," Mr. Zimmerman said.

Steve loosened the bandage.

"Hmmmmm! Not bad. Regular old-fashioned shiner. I understand you disposed of this other fellow rather efficiently."

"There wasn't much else I could do," Steve said. "He was begging for a fight, and I couldn't talk my way out of it."

"Keep that beefsteak on," Mr. Zimmerman advised. "It'll take some of the swelling away."

"I'm sorry I missed it," Yogi said. "It was just my luck to be skiing when it happened."

"You didn't miss much," Steve said. "It only lasted about three minutes."

Mr. Zimmerman got a fire going in the cook stove.

"Think you can stand a little more steak tonight?" he called in from the kitchen.

"Under my belt, yes," Steve replied.

In a few minutes the tempting odors of food drifted through the cabin.

Steve discovered that the fight had not affected his appetite. The steaks tasted wonderful, and there were beans and fried potatoes, with biscuits and honey to finish off the meal. Steve expected Yogi's father to demand an explanation of the fight, but never once did he ask why it had started. Steve admired him for that. Yogi was like his father in many ways, but when the meal was finished and they were sitting in front of the open fire, he could restrain himself no longer.

"How'd this guy happen to swing on you?" Yogi asked.

"It's a long story," Steve said. "I'm afraid it would bore your father."

"Not at all," Mr. Zimmerman said. "If you care to tell us about it, go right ahead."

Steve started by telling of the school assembly when Mr. Grossett had announced that old Central would close. He told of the reaction of the students, and of the meeting in the Beanery after school.

"I felt that the change was going to come whether we liked it or not, and the idea of a strike seemed silly to me. I tried to talk the other students out of it, and that didn't help my popularity. This fellow, Blink Kennedy, disliked my ideas so much that he started a fight with me in the Beanery. The other fellows pulled him off before I could do much about it, so really this fight started way last spring. Today was the first chance that Blink had to finish what he had started."

"And what a finish," Yogi said. "The fellow who rents skis at the lodge said you knocked him for a loop."

"I got in a lucky punch," Steve said.

Later in the evening Steve helped Yogi with the dishes, and at nine-thirty they unrolled their sleeping bags and spread them out on the bunks upstairs.

"Think you can sleep with that eye?" Mr. Zimmerman asked.

"I'll sleep okay," Steve returned. "Most of the soreness has gone out of it. I'll have to figure out a good story to tell them at school on Monday."

"Why not tell them you got in a fight?" Yogi suggested. "That would be so original nobody would believe it."

Steve was restless for a while, but finally sleep got the

upper hand and he drowsed off. He had a crazy dream about an endless line of fellows all of whom looked like Blink Kennedy. They were marching along a counter, pounding their fists and demanding service. Then his dream switched to the old Beanery across from Central High. He was standing on a stool, making a speech, but he found it difficult to keep his balance because he was wearing skis. Three fellows in the front row were also wearing skis. They resembled Skiffo Drake, Big Bill Toner, and Larry Bowman. They were shaking their fists at Steve and telling him to come outside and fight. Suddenly everybody in the room started fighting, and they were all wearing skis. This made it terribly confusing and awkward. Steve stepped to the hamburger counter with his skis. Slowly the counter started to tilt, and he was speeding downhill. Ground hamburger was flying from the tips of his skis like powdered snow. He did a snow-plow stop in the hamburger, and looked back up the counter. Everybody was pounding on the counter and demanding service. Steve woke up with a start.

He sat up in his bunk. He could still hear the pounding. He pinched himself to be sure he was awake. Somebody was pounding on the cabin door.

Mr. Zimmerman woke up at the same time. "What's that noise?" he asked.

"Sounds like someone knocking on the door," Steve said.

"I'll go down and see."

Steve reached for his flashlight and glanced at his wrist watch. It was midnight. He could hear Mr. Zimmerman on the stairs.

"Just a minute," he was shouting. "I'm coming."

The pounding stopped. Yogi's father opened the door, and Steve could hear voices, but he caught only a few of the words.

"Porcupine Ridge . . . two fellows . . . cross country . . . lost . . . last seen eight o'clock . . . ski patrol . . ."

"All right, Red," Mr. Zimmerman said. "I'll get the boys up. We'll be right over."

When the door was closed, Yogi called down to his father.

"What's the trouble, Dad?"

"Two skiers have been missing since eight o'clock. They took the Canyon Creek shortcut from Porcupine, and didn't check in at the lodge. Red Bender, of the ski patrol, is organizing a rescue party. Wants us to join them."

Yogi was out of the bunk in a bound, and Steve was right behind him. They hurried into their clothes.

"Maybe you'd better stay here," Yogi said. "That eye . . ."

"My eye is all right," Steve said. "I can see out of it. I feel okay."

Mr. Zimmerman left the decision up to Steve. He stirred the fire, and put the coffee-pot on the stove. By the time he was dressed the water was boiling.

"Better get something hot into us before we leave. Here, Steve, drink it down black."

They gulped the steaming coffee, and it left them wide awake. Steve reached for his skis and poles.

"Don't forget your flashlights," Mr. Zimmerman said.

Steve followed Yogi and his father down the path to the highway. It was still snowing. There were lights in other cabins, and it was evident that Red was assembling a large rescue party.

At least twenty men were waiting at the ski-patrol shack. It was plain that they were good skiers, for they all had fine equipment and they moved with the certainty that comes from experience. They huddled around a bonfire that the ski-patrol members had started in front of the shack. When the party had grown to about thirty, Red claimed their attention.

"Here's the dope," he said. "There were six boys in

this party. They were training for cross country, and had just left Porcupine ranger station and were heading down Silver Tip trail. Two of the boys got the bright idea of taking the Canyon Creek shortcut. They left the party against the wishes of the leader, and started out on their own. They should have reached the lodge in two hours, but they haven't been seen since they left the party. They're somewhere between the big bend on Silver Tip and the lodge. That covers a lot of territory, but we're going to comb it. They're probably injured because that shortcut is plenty rugged this time of year. We're taking two toboggans, and we'll work that area in pairs. We don't want any more casualties. That means take it easy. Everybody ready?"

Red Bender led the way, and the party started off single file. Steve and Yogi, being younger than the others, brought up the rear. Most of the men carried flashlights. The line wound slowly up the hill, and was swallowed in the darkness of the snow and the trees. Steve felt that there was something eerie about this strange procession. The bobbing lights, the heavy breathing, the soft crunch of skis on the frozen surface seemed like a part of the dream that had been interrupted by the pounding on the door. An hour ago he had been sound asleep on the cabin bunk, and now here he was trudging off into the foothills of the Cascades on a rescue mission.

When they had covered two miles the party stopped for a rest.

"How far do we have to go?" Steve asked Yogi.

"It's six miles to the big bend on the Silver Tip trail," Yogi said. "We ought to make it by two o'clock."

"Is it all uphill?"

"Most of the way. Good thing we had climbing wax."

The signal came for the party to continue, and once again the long line of bobbing lights moved forward.

The second two miles did not seem as tiring as the first. Steve was beginning to work the kinks out of his legs, and his breathing was easier. His eye bothered him a little. The cold and the snow made it smart, so he borrowed a pair of goggles from Yogi. That helped a bit.

It was after two when they reached the big bend on the trail. The timber was sparse at this elevation, and there were wide-open vistas stretching downhill to the west. When a halt was called, the party waited for instructions. Red Bender moved down the line.

"The kids left the trail somewhere along here," Red said. "We're going to spread out, and then we're all starting downhill at the same time. Two men will be responsible for about two hundred yards of territory.

Zigzag, and cover every inch of the terrain between here and Canyon Creek."

Yogi and Steve were the last two in the line so they received their instructions last.

Then Red Bender started back toward the head of the line, and in about fifteen minutes the signal was given. The rescue party started moving slowly downhill.

Steve and Yogi swung back and forth along the hillside, flashing their lights at every dark object, searching the snow for some clue to the missing skiers.

It was a long, tedious search, and there were times when Steve felt that it was hopeless. If the boys were injured they probably would not be found until daylight. If they were unharmed it was possible that they would find their own way out of the valley.

Steve wondered what Coach Hartford would think of him now. There was no question but that he was breaking a training rule, but he felt that the circumstances justified it. If he were injured and lost in the mountains he would want men searching for him just as this party was doing.

Steve kept looking for tracks in the snow, but he knew that tracks made earlier in the evening would be completely covered now. It was snowing hard, and a wind was driving up the slope, building drifts and lifting little clouds of loose snow from the ridges.

Occasionally Steve lost track of Yogi, but when he cut back he always made contact with him by flashlight or by shouting.

At three o'clock they had covered half the distance between the trail and the creek. At four-fifteen they were almost down to the floor of the valley, and no sign of the lost skiers had been found.

Steve's legs were beginning to weaken. It was tough on the legs, moving along the hillside for a hundred yards and then cutting back to move in the opposite direction. Steve wondered how he would ever get back up the slope. Perhaps if he rested—but there was no time for rest. Back and forth, back and forth! There seemed no end to this search.

As he reached the end of one cut-back, Steve noticed a particularly steep area just beyond. It had been swept clean, as if a small avalanche had taken place. He decided to explore this area, though it was beyond the limits that had been set for his search. He moved cautiously along the hillside, for there was always the danger of further slides on so steep a bank, and he had no desire to be caught in an avalanche.

Slowly he tracked along the edge of the cleared space,

flashing his light ahead, searching the fringe of the slide for some evidence of the missing skiers. There was a dark shape huddled against a tree at the base of the slide. Steve was about to pass it by, thinking it some charred stump that had been exposed by the shifting snow, when he thought he detected a slight movement. He stopped the progress of his skis and turned toward the dark lump. He approached cautiously, fearing that it might be an animal. The dim light made it difficult to see. There were bears in these hills, but generally they sensed when men were passing close to them and gave humans a wide berth. Also, if it were an animal it would be afraid of the light.

As Steve drew close he saw that the dark shape was no bear. He could make out a shattered ski and the bright red of a ski cap. The injured skier was half buried in snow.

Steve let out a shout.

"Yogi! Yogi!"

An answering shout came from the distant trees.

"Yogi! Come here, quick!"

Steve moved in close to the skier, pushed the snow aside. In the darkness he could not make out the features of the boy, but he was sure it was one of the two for whom they were looking.

A low moan came from the lips of the skier, but that

was all. Steve moved him carefully on his side, tried to straighten the leg that was bent almost double beneath him.

Yogi came struggling through the snow, puffing and snorting as he slid to a stop at Steve's side.

"This is one of them," Yogi said, bending over the boy

"The other one is probably close by," Steve said. "You go back and get the men. Have them bring the toboggans. I'll look for the other fellow."

Yogi fixed his flashlight in the crotch of a tree to serve as a marker, and then started off at full speed in the direction of the other searchers. Steve made the injured skier as comfortable as possible, and then started his cautious search around the base of the slide. The snow was rough, and branches that had been scraped from the smaller trees made the going hazardous.

Steve could not find anybody at the base of the slide, but halfway up the other side he stumbled on another limp form. This boy too was unconscious, but save for a dark splotch on the snow, and moisture on the leg of his ski pants where he had evidently jabbed himself with a ski pole, he seemed uninjured.

Steve could hear the men arriving at the other side of the slide. He shouted across the cleared space.

"Here's the other one. Give us a hand over here."

Men came scrambling to Steve's aid. Yogi was among them. Steve turned a light on the boy's face, and stepped back in surprise.

"What's the matter?" Yogi said. "Do you know him?"

Steve grinned. "Yes, I know him. This is Blink Kennedy."

LAUREL HIGH   vs.   WALLINGFORD HIGH

THE LINE-UP

Laurel High	Position	Wallingford High
Art Dressel	REL	Fred Sievers
Bud Radcliffe	RTL	Jack Larsen
Jack DeCourcey	RGL	Jay Clark
Leon Berry	C	Ralph Garton
Syd Johnson	LGR	Otto Rupp
Will Lanfield	LTR	T. Hanson
Jim Pearson	LER	George Cowan
Lou Shafer	Q	Martin Greeley
Steve Morgan	LHR	Neil Robinson
Ben Eskenazi	RHL	Jim Stevens
Phil MacLain	F	Big Bill Toner

BACK IN school Monday, Steve was the butt of a lot of jokes about his black eye. Black eyes were not uncommon during the football season, but it had been more than a week since Laurel High had played a game and consequently football could not be given as an excuse. When Steve said that he had gotten his black eye in a fight, skeptics shook their heads. There was only one way to get a black eye, they maintained, and that was to run into a door. Steve must have run into an unusually powerful door!

The Laurel eleven started its practice session on Monday with a healthy respect for the Wallingford team. Steve and the rest of the Laurel players had seen Big Bill Toner blast his way through the smaller Forest High team, and they knew what they were up against when they met the *Ducks* on the following Friday.

"Stop Big Bill," became the battle cry as the Laurel first team lined up against the second squad.

Bond, the second string fullback, who had taken such a beating the week before while playing Big Bill Toner's position, looked across the scrimmage line with apprehension in his eyes.

"Take it easy now, fellows," he pleaded. "I'm not Big Bill Toner, really. I'm just a stooge. You wouldn't hit a stooge, would you fellows, huh, would you?"

The ball was snapped. Bond had it. He scampered off tackle like a scared rabbit. Four men hit him at the scrimmage line like four heavy trucks. The thud of his body against the ground could be heard the length of the field.

"See what I mean, fellows?" he whined, as he got uncertainly to his feet. "You're taking this way too seriously. It's just a game, see? Can't we have a little more fun? Just *play* I'm Big Bill Toner."

At the end of sixty minutes Bond was still on his feet, but that's all that could be said for him. His mind was fuzzy. His body was black and blue. He was limping. His upper lip was swollen. His jersey was half torn from his shoulder.

"That's enough," Coach Hartford said. "Nice work, Bond."

"Thanks, Coach," Bond mumbled. "My only regret is that I have but one life . . ."

The following week was a hectic one for Steve Morgan. Coach Hartford drove the team relentlessly, and it was not until Thursday that the grind began to slacken. But football was not the only subject on Steve's mind. In spite of the fact that he had brushed off the fellows from Mercer High, it bothered him that they had singled him out to threaten him regarding the missing cup.

Friday morning he saw Yogi Zimmerman in the locker room. Yogi greeted him with a big grin.

"Hi, Steve."

"Where have you been all week?" Steve asked.

"Here and there," Yogi said, mysteriously.

"What's up, Yogi?"

"I've been working on the case."

"You mean the All-city cup?"

Yogi nodded.

"What have you found out?" Steve went on.

"I'm not sure yet. It's a tough case to crack, but I think I have the answer. I'll know in a week or so."

Steve felt like laughing, but Yogi was so serious that he kept his face straight. Maybe the freshman did have an idea. Yogi was such a queer little fellow that one could expect anything from him. If he wanted to play detective, there was no harm in that. But Yogi Zimmer-

Steve saw Yogi Zimmerman in the locker room

man did not look like Dick Tracy. He looked more like
Mickey Mouse.

While the teams were warming up for the game that
afternoon, Big Bill Toner sidled over to where Steve
Morgan was receiving punts. He knelt down and pre-
tended to tie his shoe, and Steve looked at him, hopeful
of a friendly greeting. Instead he got a surprise. Big Bill
Toner greeted him, it was true, but he was anything but
friendly.

"Too bad you had to gum up the works for the
Rambling Rams," Big Bill said.

"What do you mean?" Steve asked.

"You know what I mean, Morgan. Skiffo Drake,
Larry Bowman and I don't like that little deal about the
All-city cup."

"Do you really think I took that cup?" Steve asked.

"I didn't think so at first," Big Bill said, "but Skiffo
and Larry have convinced me. I even heard the story
over at Wallingford High. Everybody figures you
copped it."

"Why would I want the cup?"

"Little souvenir, maybe. Something to show your
kids."

"Don't be a dim-wit, Bill. You know I wouldn't pull a trick like that."

"I'm not sure of it. I've heard of better guys than you who turned out to be heels."

The referee's whistle interrupted the conversation. Steve joined his teammates, and he was boiling inside. He felt like punching somebody in the nose, but there were no unfriendly noses within reach. He kept his anger chained up inside. Several thoughts stirred around in his mind. The whole thing was a frame-up . . . the vicious rumor was spreading. The injustice of it rankled deep within Steve.

Coach Hartford called the Laurel team into a huddle. "This is it, fellows," he said. "If you can dump Wallingford you'll have a crack at the title. Don't forget Wallingford beat Ravenna. You'll be tied for the league lead if you take this one. It won't be easy. You have a football game on your hands."

That was evident before the first quarter was over. Wallingford played smart football. They had a heavy line, but the backfield, with the exception of Big Bill Toner, was light and fast. A young halfback named Neil Robinson was an ideal running mate for Big Bill. Robinson weighed only one forty, but he could do the hundred in ten flat. Hand him the ball and he was off like an antelope. He ran with a strange wobble to his shoulders, and he threw his hips in every direction. He was hard to tackle. Time and again he got through to the secondary, and it was up to Phil MacLain or Steve to stop him.

When Wallingford needed a few yards, Big Bill was there with the punch to put it over. Twice in the first quarter Wallingford was in scoring territory, but each time a break gave the ball to Laurel.

It was in the second quarter that Big Bill went over for a touchdown. After an exchange of punts, Wallingford brought the ball back from midfield, and after three first downs they had it on the eight-yard line. Big Bill took it on the second down, and went smashing through the Laurel line. Steve collided with him at the goal, but Big Bill fell sideways, and the ball was just across the marker.

The big zero on the scoreboard changed to a six, and Wallingford lined up for the try-for-point.

Steve walked down the Laurel line, slapping each man on the back. To Dressel, Radcliffe, and DeCourcey he said, "Get in there and block that kick." To Johnson, Lanfield, and Pearson, "Break through and smear it."

Radcliffe and Lanfield got through. They leaped high

in the air, and one of them slapped the ball down. The score remained: Wallingford 6, Laurel 0.

During the half Coach Hartford called Steve to one side.

"What was Big Bill saying to you before the game started?" Hartford asked.

"He accused me of taking the All-city cup."

"That's what I thought," the coach said. "And you blew up like a munitions dump. You haven't done a thing all half."

"I can't seem to get going."

"Did it ever occur to you," Coach Hartford said, "that he might be trying to get your goat? He knew that was a touchy subject with you. You fell for it."

"But he really means it, Coach. He said Skiffo Drake and Larry Bowman figured the same way."

"And you believed it?"

Steve nodded.

"Do you still believe it?" Hartford asked.

"I'm afraid so."

Coach Hartford turned to the second-team players who were leaning against the lockers back of the first-string squad.

"Bond," he said, "you start the second half in Morgan's position."

Bond grinned. This was more than he had expected. "Boy, am I going to work on that guy Toner," he mumbled. "I've got a little score to settle with Big Bill."

When the second half started, Steve was on the bench. He remembered how he had felt earlier in the season when the coach had benched him in the Ravenna game. Then he had felt lonely, out of place. That game had not seemed important, for he had not felt that Laurel really was his school. The other substitutes on the bench had seemed like strangers to him. But that was long ago. Now he knew every player on this bench. They were his friends. This was his team.

Steve could not account for the change that had come over him, but he was conscious of it. Now he watched every move on the field. His muscles tensed with each play. He found himself pushing against the player next to him when Bond broke through for a five-yard gain. He felt himself clenching his fists when Eskenazi fumbled on the forty-yard stripe and Wallingford High got possession of the ball.

From the stands back of the substitutes' bench came the cries of the Laurel students. Steve could sense the pent-up feeling there. The yells boomed out across the field. The whole student body was pleading with eleven men.

We want a touchdown! We want a touchdown!

Back and forth the two teams seesawed. First Laurel had an advantage; then Wallingford. For some reason Big Bill Toner was not making the yardage he had made in the first half. Then a play right in front of the bench gave Steve the answer.

Big Bill was thundering around end. He had the ball tucked firmly under his arm, and his powerful legs were churning across the sod. He had two men for interference, and he appeared to be on his way.

Then, out of nowhere, Steve caught the flash of a crimson Laurel jersey. Bond, the second-string substitute, was slashing through that interference. He went like a bowling ball through ten pins. Wham! He hit Big Bill Toner so hard that Toner left his feet, turned a somersault in the air, and landed on his shoulder beyond the sideline marker. The ball slithered from Big Bill's arms, and for a few moments football was rubbed out of his mind. When he emerged from the blackout, he shook his head and got uncertainly to his feet. He walked to his position in a fog, and before the Wallingford quarterback dared give him the ball again they had lost it on downs, and Laurel was going into a huddle.

Steve grinned to himself. That beating Bond had taken during practice scrimmage was paying off. Bond had come to hate the very name of Big Bill Toner, and he was getting his revenge.

The fourth quarter started with the score still 6 to 0 in favor of Wallingford. Steve thought that Coach Hartford might send him in when the teams changed goals, but there was no sign from Hartford that he even knew Steve was on the bench. Hartford was pacing up and down the sidelines in his usual manner, and he had eyes only for the players on the field.

With only five minutes left to play Eskenazi took a punt on the eighteen and ran it back to the thirty-five. Hartford sent a line substitute in with instructions to pass, and three passes clicked in a row.

Laurel found itself in possession of the ball on Wallingford's thirty-yard line, and the minute hand on the big clock swung past four . . . past three.

MacLain ran off tackle for eleven yards and a first down, but he was injured on the play. They had to pack him off. Hartford sent in Bartlett, a second-string half, to replace MacLain. Only nineteen yards separated the Laurel team from a score.

Now the Laurel stands were really begging for a touchdown. Their yells became a scream.

We want a touchdown!

As if in answer to their plea, Eskenazi heaved a pass

to Art Dressel, who snagged it on the eight and was downed on the five.

Two minutes left to play.

Hartford spun around, motioned to Steve.

Steve left the bench like a rocket. The coach caught him by the arm.

"Hold it," Hartford said.

Laurel was trying a line drive that piled up on the three.

"Double reverse," Hartford said in Steve's ear. "To the right."

Steve nodded. That was MacLain's play, but Mac-Lain was on the bench. Bartlett would have to carry the ball. Steve ran onto the field, replaced Bond.

In the huddle Steve passed the information to Shafer. The Laurel quarterback looked puzzled.

"You sure he said to the right?"

Steve nodded. Lou Shafer called the play.

The team lined up. On this one Steve moved to the left, took the ball from Shafer. It looked like a single reverse, but Bartlett, who had been out on a flanker, was moving fast to the right. Steve slipped the ball to him. Bartlett took it wide around Wallingford's end, and went over standing up. The score was tied—6 to 6.

There was one minute left. Laurel lined up quickly.

MacLain generally kicked the try-for-points, but Steve Morgan had to take his place. Steve was back in the kicking formation. Lou Shafer was down on one knee, arms outstretched toward the center. Leon Berry was over the ball. He looked back at Lou, eyes steady.

The ball was snapped. Lou caught it, placed it in position. Steve was stepping forward. His foot was swinging. His toe collided squarely with the ball, and the pigskin soared away over the heads of the players.

Above the crossbar, between the uprights, it sailed. The referee's hands went high above his head. The kick was good. Laurel High had won, 7 to 6.

CHAPTER TWELVE

THE TRY-FOR-POINT kick that Steve Morgan booted in the closing minutes of the game between Laurel High School and Wallingford High not only won the game for Laurel, but it focused the attention of sports writers on the broad-shouldered halfback who had played spotty football during the early season with the silver-and-crimson team.

One reporter said, "Steve Morgan, who has been either hot or cold during the first three games on the Laurel schedule, combined the two extremes yesterday when he applied a hot-foot to the pigskin with the coolness of a penguin. His kick defeated Wallingford High, and it might well be the turning point in Laurel's bid for the Portside championship."

In a column of sports comment one newspaper man wrote, "Steve Morgan had been playing against his former teammates in the first three games. Skiffo Drake, Larry Bowman, and yesterday it was Big Bill Toner. There is a psychological factor involved in this kind of

competition that may have had its effect. What Morgan does during the rest of the season remains to be seen, but there have been flashes when Steve Morgan looked like All-city material. If he settles down and plays consistent ball for the next four games he will be a hard man to replace."

Steve Morgan read the newspaper account with glowing warmth. It was the first time he had ever been mentioned for All-city selection. But even if he was considered for the team there was still the shadow of the missing trophy hanging over him. Until that mystery was cleared, Steve felt that his chances of making the honor eleven were slim.

Steve looked for Yogi Zimmerman in the locker room on Monday morning, but the freshman was nowhere to be seen. When the absence sheet came around during the second period Steve noticed that Yogi's name was on the list. Consequently, he was surprised when he found Yogi munching a hamburger in the lunchroom at noon.

"Where were you this morning?" Steve asked, as he placed his tray on the table and pulled up a stool at Yogi's side.

"I've been visiting."

"What do you mean, 'visiting'?"

"Mercer High," was Yogi's laconic reply.

"Don't tell me you've been skipping all morning."

"Technically, no. I've been away from classes, if that's what you mean."

"How will you get away with it?" Steve asked.

"I won't. They'll hand me ten or twelve demerits. I'll work 'em off after school in the make-up room."

"And why, may I ask, did you visit Mercer High?"

"Special investigation," Yogi said with an air of importance.

"Were you checking up on the Owls?"

"Could be. Remember that fellow in the stag shirt? His name is Chuck Holmes. He's not a bad guy."

"What makes you think so?" Steve asked.

"He's willing to play ball."

Steve looked at Yogi out of the corner of his eyes. The freshman was busy working on his second hamburger, and he was washing it down with a double-size cola.

"Okay," Steve said. "Spill it. I'm dying to hear."

"Well," Yogi gulped, "these Mercer Owls were going to beat you up if you didn't produce the cup. I've fixed that. They're giving us more time."

"You 'fixed' it?"

"Sure. I told 'em I'd produce the cup by the end of the season if they would lay off."

"And just how will you produce the cup?" Steve asked.

"I haven't figured that out yet."

Steve took a deep breath. He stifled a growing desire to put his big hands around Yogi's little neck and squeeze.

Yogi grinned. "I know just how you feel, Steve. There are times when I could choke you, too."

"There are?" Steve said, surprise in his voice. "Like when, for instance?"

"Like when you stood around on your flat feet in the first half of the Wallingford game and let Big Bill Toner make a fool out of you."

"He didn't make a fool out of me," Steve protested.

"He certainly did. He had you buffaloed—hypnotized. I was about ready to give you up as a hopeless job. Then you booted that try-for-point. That saved your skin, Steve. If you had missed that one I would have washed my hands of you."

"I'm glad I made it," Steve said humbly.

"You ought to be, because without me you'd be a dead duck as far as All-city is concerned."

"And just how are you going to make an All-city player out of me?"

"Like this," Yogi said, hunching his shoulders and sliding his chair closer to Steve. "This Saturday we play Airport High. Airport is a set-up. You're going to be in there from the first kickoff, and for sixty minutes you're going to be playing more football than you ever played before in one hour. You're going to be every-where. Packin' the ball, catching passes, running down punts, blocking, tackling. Every time the whistle blows you're going to be on the bottom of the pile. You're going to be . . ."

"Wait a minute. Hold it," Steve said. "That's a big order."

Yogi grinned. "You get the general idea?"

Steve nodded. "Okay, Yogi. I'll try."

Steve Morgan tried. When Laurel High played Airport High the following Saturday, it was Steve who sparked the team from the opening kickoff until the final gun. He was in on every play, and when he wasn't carrying the ball himself he was tearing big holes in the Airport line for his teammates to scamper through.

Coach Hartford sat on the Laurel bench and smiled to himself. For the first time Steve Morgan was showing the form that the coach expected of him. But what pleased Hartford more than anything else was that he played sixty minutes of consistent football. Never once did he let down. Never once did he make a misplay. He was cool and tireless—always driving—and the rest of the Laurel team caught the spirit of his play. Dressel and Pearson, the Laurel ends, were down on punts. Radcliffe and Lanfield, the tackles, were smashing through to smear the Airport backfield behind the line of scrimmage. Eskenazi, Lou Shafer, and Phil MacLain showed power on offense. Laurel High was clicking.

Coach Hartford knew one reason why his team had switched form. There were no former players from Old Central on the Airport team. The Phantom Backfield bugaboo that had hung over Steve in the first three games was removed in this contest with Airport. His movements were free, unrestricted. He played with a seemingly reckless abandon that gave a natural coordination to his arms and legs. It was as if chains had been removed, and Steve Morgan was free at last.

The score when the timekeeper's gun ended the game was Laurel High 36, Airport High 0.

"Now we're going places," Yogi Zimmerman said the following Monday when he met Steve in the locker room. "You looked like a football player Saturday. Three more games like that, and it's in the bag."

"Mercer High won't be such a set-up," Steve pointed out. "Mercer High tied Wallingford."

"Sure, but that has nothing to do with it. The idea is to run 'em ragged. Somebody has to lose, and it might as well be Mercer. With a few breaks we could win the city championship, Steve. Ravenna plays Hilltop this week, and if Hilltop wins, that will leave us leading the league. We'll be the only team with one defeat."

"Do you think we can win the next three?" Steve was serious. He had learned to respect this little freshman's opinion.

"Why not?" Yogi demanded. "You have the whole school pulling for you. Did you hear the yelling at the Airport game? The student body is backing you to a man."

Steve pulled his books out of the locker and checked his notebook to be sure he had the paper due in chemistry class. Yogi Zimmerman's words were soaking in. *The whole school is backing you to a man.* As Steve walked down the hall he noticed that most of the pupils had a friendly grin for him.

"Hiya, Steve!" one sophomore called.

"Nice going, Steve," the Boys' Club President said.

Greetings were on every side. This was almost like old Central. There he knew everybody. Here he was learning to know everybody. He walked up the stairs with Syd Johnson.

"Do you know, Syd," Steve said, "I have a confession to make. When you and I left old Central I didn't think any other school could take its place. Of course, Laurel hasn't really taken its place, but I'm beginning to feel as though Laurel was my school, too."

"I know what you mean," Syd replied. "I suppose we'll always have a warm spot in our hearts for old Central, but maybe there's room for two warm spots. I'm beginning to like Laurel myself. I had a funny feeling of pride when we started to roll against Airport. A fellow can't put it in words—it's just inside him, that's all."

There was a "pep" assembly before the Mercer game, and Steve Morgan sat with two or three other football players in the back of the auditorium. He was used to assemblies now. It no longer seemed strange to him to sit in the big auditorium, and the yells that had sounded queer when he first heard them were beginning to have a familiar ring.

Steve joined in two or three lively songs with the band, and he enjoyed the singing. The Laurel band was a good band, and there was a catchy swing to their playing. Steve found himself tapping his feet in time to the music.

After the cheer leaders had led a few yells, Coach Hartford was introduced. The coach came on the stage wearing a sweat shirt and baggy trousers. His hair looked as if it had been combed hastily, and when he stood at the microphone, smiling, the students gave him a big hand.

Coach Hartford was well liked at Laurel. In two short months he had won the respect and admiration of the entire student body. Considering the fact that he had come from a rival school, that was a difficult thing to do, but his reputation as a coach had preceded him and he had the personality to go with it.

"I don't know why they asked me to make a talk," Hartford began. "The fellows on the team will tell you that I make a pretty good speech down in the locker room, but when I get up here in front of a mike my vocabulary doesn't seem adequate.

"They asked me to talk about the Mercer game, but I'd rather wait until that game is over before I do any talking. Instead, I'm going to say a few words about the Laurel student body. You've done a great job so far this season, and if you keep backing your team right up to the end, we have a fighting chance of winning the title. Of course, anything can happen in football, and a coach is foolish to make predictions regarding his players, but there's nothing in the book that says he can't predict things about the student body, so here goes. I predict that you come through this season like a championship student body, and that means your enthusiasm and behavior will be tops, and that your attitude will be good whether we win or lose. I hope we win."

Coach Hartford left the stage with cheers ringing. The band struck up the school song, and the pupils shouted the words: "*Forward, forward, forward Laurel High . . .*"

Next the yell team escorted Penny Carson out to the center of the stage. Penny Carson was rapidly winning a place for herself at Laurel High. She had been given a part in the Senior Play, and she had been chosen to serve on the Advisory Board. The students knew her, and cheered her entrance.

"At old Central," and Penny smiled, "we used to have girls on the yell team. For two years I helped lead the yells in that school, but since I've come to Laurel all I can do is follow the boys."

The students laughed, and the yell team clapped their hands.

"But seriously, I've grown to love Laurel High. When I first came here I thought that would never be possible, but everyone has been so grand to me that I just couldn't help it."

Syd Johnson dug his elbow into Steve Morgan's side.

"Penny is joining us," he whispered.

Steve nodded.

"At old Central," Penny went on, "we used to have a yell called the war chant. It was a simple yell. It went: *Fight 'em, Rams, Fight 'em*, and we kept repeating it, each time a little louder, until we reached the limit. You know what I mean. We could give the same yell here, and use the name *Hawks*. How about it?"

"Let's go," someone shouted.

"All right," Penny said, stretching her arms. "Ready! Hit it!"

Fight 'em, Hawks, Fight 'em!
FIGHT 'EM, HAWKS, FIGHT 'EM!

The Laurel student body joined in wholeheartedly, and by the time they had repeated the line ten times the auditorium was filled with more noise than ever before.

Penny ran from the stage, laughing, and the audience screeched its approval.

Steve paid little attention to the rest of the program. He was thinking of Penny leading that yell. The last time he had heard her lead the *War Chant* was in the Beanery across from old Central. Then she had been trying to stir up the student body to strike. Now she was using the yell for a different purpose. Laurel had to beat Mercer High: Penny wanted Laurel to win.

CHAPTER THIRTEEN

THE GAME with Mercer High was not as one-sided as the Airport game had been, but it was obvious that the Laurel squad had found a new determination—a new drive. They played with the same skill, but they were up against a stronger opponent. This time they were able to win by only thirteen points, and Mercer pushed over a touchdown in the second quarter to make the final score Laurel 20, Mercer 7.

The following week Yogi Zimmerman presented Steve with a new picture taken during the Mercer game.

"I made it from the sidelines, with a telephoto lens," Yogi said, beaming. "Pretty good, don't you think?"

"It's perfect," Steve said, admiring the picture. He was in the act of kicking a punt. Yogi had enlarged the picture and cropped it so that Steve's figure stood out sharply and clearly. A professional photographer could not have done better.

"You ought to make a business of this, Yogi," Steve said.

"Give me time," Yogi replied. "I told you I was training to be a news photographer. If you ever want any pictures taken just let me know."

Steve looked around cautiously, and when he spoke his voice was low.

"Yogi, did you see that girl leading the yell at the assembly Friday?"

"Yeah," Yogi said, entering into the spirit of conspiracy.

"How about snapping her picture in the hall sometime? On the quiet, I mean. So she won't know."

"Why, Steve!" Yogi exclaimed. "You didn't tell me you had a heart throb at Laurel."

"Heart throb, my eye! I just want a picture of the girl, see, and if you breathe it to a soul I'll tie you up in little knots and sell you for a puzzle."

"It's as good as snapped," Yogi said. "Leave it to me."

Two days later Yogi presented Steve with an enlarged picture of Penny Carson. She was standing in the window of the third floor alcove, and there was a pensive look on her face. It made Steve think of the day he had stood in that alcove after his meeting with Larry Bowman.

"You sure she didn't see you take this?" Steve asked.

"Absolutely. When I take a candid shot I'm the only one who knows it."

"Yogi, you're wonderful."

"I'm glad somebody else thinks so. Until now I was afraid I was the only one who ever had such an idea."

That evening Steve put Penny's picture on his dresser. He tried to study chemistry, but he found his gaze shifting to the picture every few minutes. It was distracting having Penny's likeness there, for each time he looked at her his mind wandered back to some pleasant memory of old Central. Steve had never gone "steady" with Penny, but they had been together frequently at dances and on house parties. Penny was a smooth dancer, and she was always ready for a swim, or a game of tennis, or a sail on the lake in Steve's flattie.

Sailing was one of Penny's favorite sports. Dressed in a pair of levis that were rolled above her knees, and wearing a loose crew-neck sweater, she was at home on the water. Her shoulder-length auburn hair whipped in the breeze, and her laughing eyes were bluer than the sky over the Cascades. She could trim a jib or maneuver the flattie from a port to starboard tack with the skill of a veteran. She was never awkward in a boat. With her bare feet planted firmly on the little forward deck, and her hand on the halyard, she looked as if she were a member of the crew, and she was a member of the crew when she and Steve leaned far over the side to help the frail craft hold her footing in a stiff breeze.

Steve remembered those days with a feeling of nostalgia. It was evident that they were gone forever, for since the last days of old Central Penny had shown no interest in him. It had never occurred to Steve that he might have been to blame for this state of affairs. It had never occurred to him until this night as he sat looking at her picture. Perhaps he had been at fault. He had never asked her to go sailing again. He had never asked her to accompany him to a dance. He had just taken it for granted that the fun they had shared had come to an end when old Central had died.

He stretched out on his bed and folded his hands under his head. For a long time he lay staring at the ceiling. Yes, he had been a dope. The conclusion came with shocking suddenness. Perhaps if he asked Penny to a dance she would accept. If he broke the ice it might be that they could recapture some of the carefree good times they had enjoyed at old Central.

Steve sat up on the edge of his bed and glanced at his wrist watch. It was only nine thirty. That was not too late to call. In three weeks there was to be a big dance at the Yacht Club after the All-city banquet. If he asked Penny now, tonight, she might accept.

He started to rise, and then sank back on the bed weakly. For a moment he had forgotten about the All-city trophy. That had been the real cause of the unfriendliness shown by the old Central gang. Penny would never go to the dance with him as long as the finger of suspicion pointed at him. If he asked her and she refused, it would only add to his humiliation.

The hand on his wrist watch moved toward ten. Slowly he was mustering courage to call Penny on the phone. Why should he be humiliated? He had not stolen the trophy. His conscience was clear. He should stand up and assert himself. Penny would never go to the dance with him if he failed to ask her. It was his move.

He put his feet on the floor, then sat for several minutes on the edge of the bed, studying Penny's picture. It occurred to him that he should be studying chemistry, but he brushed the thought aside. He argued with himself. It was too late to call a girl. But it was only ten o'clock; that was not late. If he postponed asking her now somebody else would beat him to it. He wanted to be at that dance. Everybody would be at the Yacht Club dance. He wanted to ask Penny.

He went to the head of the stairs and listened. His

sister was in her room and his father and mother were in the living room listening to the news on the radio. The phone was in the kitchen. Slowly he made his way downstairs.

Steve closed the kitchen door quietly, and went to the phone. He looked for Penny's number, then paused with his finger in the dial. Should he call her? Why not? This was as good a time as any. He started to dial the number.

When he had finished he could hear the phone ringing at the other end. He thought of hanging up, but he was too slow. A voice answered.

"Hello, Penny?" Steve asked.

"Just a minute, please. I'll call Penny."

Steve realized then that it was her mother who had answered. As he waited, he was aware of a strange constriction in his throat and chest. His throat felt tight. He wondered if he could talk. He would be smart if he put the receiver on the hook and forgot the whole thing. He started to hang up, but just then a girl's voice sounded at the other end of the line.

"Hello?"

"Hello," Steve said. "Is that you, Penny?"

"Yes."

"This is Steve Morgan."

Steve thought he could hear the catch in Penny's voice.

"Oh . . . yes," she said. "What is it, Steve?"

"I was just thinking," Steve continued, "that it would be swell if you would go to the Yacht Club dance with me after the All-city banquet. Maybe we could . . ."

"I'm sorry, Steve," Penny interrupted. "If you had only called sooner it would have been fun, but you see, I already have a date."

Steve had a sinking feeling.

"That's too bad . . . I mean, that's okay, Penny. Sorry I didn't call sooner. Maybe next time."

"Maybe next time . . ." Penny repeated.

"Well, thanks just the same, Penny. So long."

Steve put the receiver on the hook, and for a moment sat staring at the mouthpiece. His forehead felt moist. His lips were drawn into a firm line. Well, he had asked for it. She had brushed him off as gently as possible. He was a dope, all right. He should never have called.

The contest with Islandview High was just another game on the Laurel schedule. Steve Morgan led his team to a 21 to 0 victory, and then the crimson-and-silver team went into two weeks of training for the Thanksgiving Day game with Forest High.

There was little to do but drill against the Forest plays. Coach Hartford was satisfied with his offense. In the last three games Laurel High had piled up a total of 77 points to their opponents' 7, and no high school coach in the Portside league could ask for more. Now if Laurel could get over this final hurdle the city title would be wrapped and delivered to the Crimson *Hawks*.

But to Coach Hartford and Steve Morgan there was more at stake than the winning of the city championship. To Steve, the success of the Laurel team and the place he had made for himself in a new school were partial justification of the stand he had taken back at Central High when the students had threatened to strike. It had not been easy to take the unpopular side in the controversy over the closing of the school. It had caused the breach between himself and other members of the *Rambling Rams*. It had been largely responsible for the rumor that he had stolen the All-city cup. It had strained his friendship with pupils who had grown up with him through grade school.

To Coach Hartford there was satisfaction in seeing eleven young men playing together with the precision of a machine. This team had been a balky machine in the beginning, and there were times when the coach wondered if he would ever get all the parts working together. That first defeat at the hands of Ravenna High had really been the turning point. Had Laurel won that game they might have lost the championship. Such things happen in football, and it is only at the end of the season that a coach can look back and analyze the moves that spell failure or success.

So the Laurel team was ready for Forest High—ready physically and psychologically. This was Laurel's day. It was in the air. It was apparent in the confident cheers that rolled down over the field from the Laurel rooting section. It was in the frisky antics of the Laurel players as they warmed up before the game. They kicked, passed, and ran up and down the field with the spirit of real champions.

The referee called the two captains together. Steve Morgan approached, helmet in hand. He shook hands with Tucker, who wore the dark-green jersey of the Forest High *Timberwolves*. When the coin flipped in the air, Steve won the toss.

Sports writers in the press box jotted down notes: Laurel High will defend the west goal. Forest High will kick off.

A radio announcer spoke into his microphone: "It's a WONDerful day here in Portside. The sun is shining brilliantly as these two colorful teams line up on the

Civic Field for the start of a game that will determine the city championship. The crimson-and-silver *Hawks* of Laurel High will receive at the west end of the field, and the green-clad *Wolves* of Forest High will kick off. The two teams are lining up now. The referee is ready to blow his whistle. There it goes! It's a long, high kick, floating far down the field to the waiting arms of Steve Morgan, Laurel halfback.

"Steve Morgan has the ball now," the announcer continued. "He is past the twenty . . . the thirty. He is slanting across the field. Two tacklers had their hands on him but they missed. He is getting wonderful blocking. Over the forty . . . the forty-five . . . the fifty. Steve Morgan has reversed his field. Hold everything, folks . . . he's in Forest territory. Wonderful footwork! He cuts back . . . dodges two tacklers . . . he's across the thirty-five . . . the thirty . . . there he goes . . . like a galloping ghost . . . he's turning on the speed . . . he's in the clear . . . the twenty . . . the ten . . . the five . . . he's over. Wow! *What* a run . . . ninety yards . . . right through the entire Forest team for a touchdown . . . and the game is only one minute old . . . Laurel leads, 6 to 0 . . . and the stands have gone wild. Can you hear those kids yelling? That's their boy who did that. Steve Morgan is his name. You're going to hear more of this fellow Morgan, folks, and now, while I catch my breath, stand by. I'll repeat the story of that sensational opening run."

The radio listeners heard a good deal more about Steve

Morgan before the game was over, and the people in the stands saw him scamper down the field for two more touchdowns before the last whistle blew. Forest High made one touchdown on an intercepted pass in the second quarter, but the final score was 21 to 6 in favor of Laurel.

In the locker room after the game Coach Hartford shook hands with each of his players. When he came to Steve Morgan a smile dodged along his lips. Words were unnecessary. Gratitude was in his eyes.

When Steve was dressed he found Yogi Zimmerman waiting outside the locker room.

"You were great, Steve."

"Don't forget the other fellows," Steve said. "It takes more than a halfback to win a ball game."

"Sure, but ten players don't make a football team, either. It takes a full team, and you were the eleventh man. You're in, Steve. You're a cinch for All-city."

"I'm not so sure of that," Steve said.

CHAPTER FOURTEEN

From the newspaper accounts that followed the Forest High game it looked as if Yogi Zimmerman might be right again. There was much talk of Steve Morgan as a candidate for the All-city, but Steve knew that the newspaper men did not choose the members of the honor team. That was left to the coaches. It was true that favorable publicity helped influence the coaches in their choice, but the season was half over before Steve began to get the attention that would mark him for recognition. Another candidate whose playing had been consistent throughout the entire season could easily win the nod from impartial judges.

Steve Morgan was certain of one thing. His playing in the Forest High game had made him a hero in the eyes of his schoolmates. When he arrived at school on Monday he received congratulations on every side. Fellows who had never noticed him before came up to slap him on the back, and to tell him he had played a fine game. Even members of the faculty stopped him in the hall to talk about the game. It made Steve feel good. It made him feel as if he were really a part of Laurel High.

There was an awards assembly on Wednesday, and Coach Hartford called his players on the stage to present them with their letters.

It was the first time Steve Morgan had appeared on the Laurel stage, and he was nervous. He waited in the wings while the linemen shuffled out ahead of him. When his name was called he was greeted by a roar of applause. Grinning sheepishly, Steve took his place on the platform.

"I'm proud of you fellows," Coach Hartford said, when the entire team was assembled. "You have come through the season with only one defeat, and your record is the best in the city. You have won the Portside championship, and you deserve it. Early in the season there were times when your playing was a little ragged, but many of you were strangers to the school, and you were under a handicap. It is a credit to all of you that you found yourselves. You developed into a smooth outfit, and you reached your peak last Saturday when you played Forest High. I tell you, I got a real thrill when you started clicking, and I believe every student in Laurel High is as proud of you as I am." The coach turned to the audience. "How about it, gang?"

The cheer that rang through the auditorium of Laurel High was real evidence of how the student body felt. The pupils whistled, stamped their feet, and their cries of "Yea! Team!" clapped like thunder from the balcony and the main floor.

Steve felt a queer tingle creeping along his spine. It was similar to that first faint thrill he had experienced after the Hilltop game. He had fought against the feeling then, but there was no fighting this strange new thrill. It was in his blood. It would not be denied. At last he had found his place at Laurel High. This was his school. They were cheering for him, and for his teammates. The little cold wave that pricked across his scalp was a part of his response. This elation—this sense of well-being—was his reward, and Steve knew that such a moment as this was worth all of the effort, all of the back-breaking grind that had gone into the football season.

Coach Hartford was presenting the letters now—a crimson "L" on a background of silver. Steve knew that he would wear the letter with pride. It stood for something that was hard to define. It represented the cheers of a united student body. It stood for the building, the faculty, all of the friends he had made since he left old Central. It was a symbol of something intangible—a school spirit that he had helped to create. It stood for the implicit faith of little freshmen like Yogi Zimmerman. It was the insignia for a new loyalty, discovered by seniors who had come grudgingly up the steps of Laurel High only to find that this school, too, had a heart that was big and ready to receive them. Steve shook hands with Coach Hartford and accepted his letter. It was a bond with Laurel High that he would never be able to break.

When the assembly was over, Syd Johnson and Steve left the stage together.

"We made it, Steve." Syd grinned.

"Yeah," Steve replied. "There were times when I thought we were going to foul everything up, but somehow it worked out."

"There isn't much left now but the banquet."

"I kind of dread the banquet," Steve said.

"No sense in that. You have a good chance of making the team."

"I don't figure it that way. Too many good backfield men around town. You linemen ought to rate All-city. You were the fellows who opened the holes."

"Not a chance," Syd said. "Erickson of Hilltop, Peeler of Ravenna, Eaton of Hilltop . . . those boys are a cinch. Then there's Yoder, of Forest High. He'll be in there."

"And there isn't a single one among them who could push a fellow named Johnson around."

"Applesauce. If I make All-city it will be somebody's mistake."

"It would be a pretty good mistake, if you ask me."

They had reached the landing on the way to the second floor. Students were crowding up and down the stairway. There were shouts of approval as Steve and Syd pushed through the throng. "Hiya, Steve! Hiya, Syd!" Even the girls smiled their recognition.

"Let's get out of this crowd," Steve said.

"Okay. Show me how."

Steve led Syd to the alcove on the third floor. There was no rush here.

"Let's take a breather," Steve said. "We have five minutes to get to class."

"Good idea," Syd said.

They sat down on the window seat, and stretched their legs out in front of them.

"Are you going to the Yacht Club dance after the banquet?" Steve asked.

"Yeah. Are you?"

"Guess not."

"How come? Everybody will be there."

"No date," Steve said.

"Did you try to get one?"

"Yeah." Steve wished Syd would change the subject.

"An' you give up with one try," Syd said scornfully. "What's the matter with you? There're hundreds of girls around here who would swoon if you asked them."

"I don't want any swooners. I just want a smooth dancer, and it wouldn't hurt if she was good-looking."

"Tell you what," Syd said. "My girl friend has a friend . . ."

"No you don't," Steve interrupted. "I've been taken before. I'm off blind dates."

"But wait a minute. This gal has class. She's from out of town."

"No thanks," Steve said, shaking his head.

"She was Queen of the Forest Festival at Shelton."

"What? What did you say?"

"I said she was Queen of the Forest Festival. She can dance like a dream. According to Joan, several movie scouts have been trailing her."

"And you mean I could get a date with this . . . this Queen?"

"Sure. She's coming to visit Joan, and if I don't find a date for her, Joan can't go to the dance."

"That sort of puts you on the spot," Steve said.

"I'll say."

"I hate to see you in a jam, Syd. After all, you're an

old friend of mine. I might . . . I might take this Queen just as a favor to you."

"Would you, Steve?"

"Just as a favor, understand?"

"I'll never be able to repay you."

"Aw, forget it."

In his trigonometry class, Steve found it difficult to concentrate on the work being outlined on the blackboard. His mind was like the chalk compass his teacher was using. It kept going around in circles. His thoughts always returned to the starting place—the football dance. At the end of the period he knew little more trigonometry than when he had entered the classroom, but he had done some heavy thinking.

He had accepted a blind date. That was against all the rules and regulations he had set up for himself. But then, perhaps this blind date would be different. Her name was Queen Barbara V. That was all Steve knew. She was a friend of Joan's and she was good-looking. She would have to be pretty, Steve reasoned, or they would never have selected her to be Queen of the Forest Festival. She might even be beautiful. Well, that remained to be seen. A fellow had to have a girl if he was going to this dance, and Steve wanted to be present. He knew that all of the football players in Portside would be there. Besides, there was the little matter of Penny Carson. Steve was not a vindictive person, but if Penny Carson should see him at the dance with a beautiful girl she would be greatly impressed. Steve smiled to himself. He hoped Queen Barbara was a knock-out.

When Steve entered the locker room at the end of the day he was still feeling pretty good. Yogi Zimmerman was waiting for him.

"You look as if your troubles were over," Yogi said. "What's the big grin for?"

"Am I grinning?" Steve said. "Pardon it, please."

"I suppose it's because of that new letter they handed you this morning. Think you're pretty good, don't you?"

"Nobody but you could talk like that and not get punched in the nose," Steve said, rumpling the freshman's hair. "The truth is, Yogi, I do think I'm pretty good. I'm stepping out with a Queen."

"You mean that you and Penny have made up?"

"No," Steve said, his tone changing. "Penny and I have not made up. And Yogi, if you're a smart boy, you'll keep your little freckled nose out of my social affairs."

"I'm sorry," Yogi said. "I didn't mean to be nosey."

"How are we coming on the case of the stolen trophy?" Steve asked, to change the subject.

Yogi's shoulders sagged.

"I'm afraid I'm not much of a detective," he admitted. "I've been working on it right along, but all my clues lead up blind alleys. I still have a couple of hunches left, though," he said, brightening. "Perhaps we can crack the case before the All-city banquet."

"How are those fellows from Mercer High making out?" Steve asked.

"I talked to Chuck Holmes last week," Yogi said. "His gang is getting a little impatient. I promised them I would produce the trophy by the end of the season, and I haven't done it."

"Well, if they want to make something of it, let them."

"It isn't that, Steve. I know you can take care of yourself. It's just that I hate to let you down."

"You haven't let me down, Yogi. You're one of the best friends I ever had."

Yogi's shoulders straightened. His voice was determined.

"One of these days I'll clear up that mess for you, or my name isn't Yogi Zimmerman."

CHAPTER FIFTEEN

THE BANQUET at the Athletic Club was an annual affair. It was attended by the players and coaches of the Port-side teams and by the local sports writers. G. N. Baker, the Superintendent of Schools, was the master of cere-monies. Though the state championship game was yet to be played, this banquet was something of a climax, com-ing as it did at the end of the season. Until the program was over nobody would know who had been chosen for the All-city team.

There were eight tables in the big dining room at the Athletic Club—one for each of the high schools in Port-side. Steve sat at the Laurel table and looked around at his teammates. They were wearing their best suits, white shirts, and neckties. They looked strange with neckties, as if they had suddenly grown from boys to men. Lou Shafer ran his finger around inside his collar and mum-bled, "Whew!"

The food was good, and there was plenty for every-one. Steve would have enjoyed it more had not the gathering reminded him of the missing trophy and the suspicions that had been directed at him. The presence of Skiffo Drake, Big Bill Toner, and Larry Bowman at the other tables made him uneasy. He knew how they felt toward him. If only Yogi Zimmerman had succeeded in finding the silver cup this banquet might have been more pleasant. But that was not the case. Yogi Zimmerman had failed and so had Steve, for the mystery of the stolen cup was still unsolved.

As the meal progressed, Steve noticed that Skiffo Drake was darting quick glances at him. He could almost read what was going on in Skiffo's mind. Skiffo was wondering if Steve Morgan would make the All-city, and he was also wondering just what effect such a choice would have on their chances for the state championship. It was written all over his face. When Steve caught him in one of these searching glances, Skiffo turned away hurriedly, almost in embarrassment.

Big Bill Toner never looked in Steve's direction. His head was down over his plate during most of the meal, and Steve wondered what thoughts were churning in his mind.

Larry Bowman ignored Steve completely. He was the life of the party at the Hilltop table, laughing and joking and making wisecracks at the expense of his teammates.

Larry was a good-looking boy, and dressed in a white shirt and with his hair combed back, he appeared almost collegiate. There was no doubt about his popularity. The fellows who sat at his table competed with one another for his attention, and Larry was quick to acknowledge every bid for recognition.

There was entertainment during the meal. A piano player from Airport High beat out some smooth boogie woogie. A pretty girl from Wallingford High sang three plaintive tunes in a manner that showed the Dinah Shore influence. A double quartette from Forest High developed a little close harmony on several numbers from the Hit Parade. By the time dessert was served everybody was in a jovial mood—everybody but Steve Morgan. Steve was nervous. He kept biting his lip, running his hand through his hair, and changing his position. He wished the evening were over. He almost hoped that his name would not be mentioned for the All-city. It would be easier that way. With less publicity, less acclaim, people might forget the incident of the missing trophy. As long as he was in the public eye there would be former pupils from Central High who would look at him queerly, accusingly. Had Steve been less sensitive he might have put up a callous front to whispered accusations, but that was not his nature. Steve had feelings that were close to the surface, and a questioning look from a classmate could cut like the keen edge of a blade. It was such a look that Steve saw in Skiffo Drake's eyes.

Finally, when the chairs had been pushed back and the tables cleared, Superintendent Baker got to his feet. He introduced the Mayor of Portside, the president of the Athletic Club, and the football coach from the State University. Each of these men made a short talk that had a familiar theme—good sportsmanship, and the value of athletics to the growing boy. Steve wished that they would hurry along to the main business of the evening. Every boy in the room was curious about the All-city, and they were growing restless. The clock over the speakers' table pointed to eight-thirty. At nine-thirty Steve and Syd were to call for the girls who would accompany them to the dance at the Yacht Club.

Steve nudged Syd in the ribs and whispered. "When are they going to get it over?"

"Search me," Syd said. "Why don't you relax, Steve?"

"I can't. I keep worrying about that dance. Do you think the girls will wait for us?"

"Guess they'll have to. We're going in my car."

"This could go on forever. You sure that friend of Joan's arrived from Shelton?"

Syd nodded. "Saw her this afternoon. She's really a queen, and I mean *Queen*."

"If she isn't I'll never forgive you, Syd."

"Don't worry. She's one hundred per cent."

When the last of the speakers had finished, Superintendent Baker stood up.

"It is my pleasure to announce," he said, "that the Coach's Association has unanimously selected Coach Hartford of Laurel High to direct the All-city team in its post-season game against the All-state team. Coach Pete Slade, of Wallingford High, will be his assistant."

There were cheers and handclapping throughout the room.

"And now, Coach Hartford, will you please come forward to announce the selection of the All-city team?"

Hartford walked to the platform. He made a little speech thanking his associates for choosing him to coach the All-city. Then he pulled a sheet of paper from his pocket and started to read the names of the players who had made the honor eleven.

"For the left-end position the coaches have chosen Don Erickson, from Hilltop High."

Don Erickson stood up while the other players applauded. There was a big smile on his face.

"Come up here, Don," Hartford said. "We want this team on the platform."

"Nice going, Don," someone shouted as the Hilltop end walked to the platform.

Hartford read the other line selections.

"Jim Eaton, of Hilltop, left tackle."

There was a big cheer from the Hilltop table. That was two linemen their team had placed on the All-city. Steve recalled that the left side of the Hilltop line was strong. Very little yardage was made around Erickson and Eaton.

Hartford's voice continued. "Brad Peeler, of Ravenna, left guard."

This time it was Ravenna's turn to lead in the cheering. Peeler was fast on his feet for a stocky man. He was always a good, dependable guard.

"For center," Coach Hartford announced, "the coaches have chosen Orin Wagner, from Airport High."

The players at the Airport table went wild. It was the first time in three years that one of their number had made the All-city. Little Airport High was generally trampled on by the larger schools, but they did not trample on Orin Wagner. He played steady, consistent ball. In fact, everybody acknowledged that he was the bulwark of the Airport line.

"For right guard," Coach Hartford said, "we have chosen a man who has played all season at left guard, but he was too good to pass up. Syd Johnson, from Laurel High."

"Hurrah!" Steve shouted. It was a spontaneous outburst, but it was soon drowned by the general applause. He had hoped Syd Johnson would make the team, and now it was a certainty. He slapped Syd on the shoulder, and the whole Laurel team stood up and clapped as Syd made his way to the platform.

"For right tackle, the choice is Tad Brownlee, from Forest High."

Tad was a big, strapping fellow, with a good-natured grin and shoulders a mile wide. He had done a fine job for Forest High throughout the season, and this was his reward.

"For right end the vote goes to Chuck Mallet, from Mercer High."

There was a line! Every man in the room was conscious of the fact that the selections were well made. Fast, strong, powerful—the All-city team ought to go places with that forward wall. There might be other good players on the second team, but these men were outstanding. They deserved the honor they had received.

"Now we come to the backfield," Coach Hartford said. "The four men I am about to name received the unanimous vote of all the coaches in the city. First we have Skiffo Drake, right half for Ravenna High."

The cheers echoed throughout the room. Skiffo Drake had danced his way onto the All-city. He was a flashy player, a tough man to tackle, and a speed demon on offense. Steve applauded with the rest. He knew that Skiffo had it coming. He had it coming ever since that first game of the year when Ravenna defeated Laurel. All through the season Skiffo had played the same brand of ball—"brilliant" was the word the sports writers used.

"For quarterback, the nod goes to Larry Bowman, from Hilltop High."

A big shout went up from the Hilltop players. That was three men from their school on the All-city. Larry Bowman was a good quarterback. He had demonstrated that in every game. Cool, quick, determined, he had led his team through a lot of trouble, and his team had not fared too badly. Hilltop was third in the league standings.

"In the fullback spot we have selected Big Bill Toner, from Wallingford High."

Wallingford had been rather neglected on this team, but they made up for it when Big Bill's name was announced. He was a stand-out for the fullback's position. No other fullback in the city had made the showing Big Bill had made. He was a cinch for the job.

While Big Bill was making his way to the platform, Steve sat in his chair and gripped the arms so tightly that his knuckles stood out in white rows across the back of his hand. There was only one position left. He felt his throat muscles tighten. He gulped, but he tried to appear calm. Others might look at him, but they would never know how he felt inside.

"At left half——" Hartford paused, and Steve was sure his heart missed a beat. "At left half," he repeated, "we have Steve Morgan, from Laurel High."

Somehow, Steve got to his feet. The room seemed to be whirling around. He could see faces, but they looked blurred. He could hear applause, but it seemed distant. He steadied himself on the back of his chair.

When he was sure he could make it, he walked to the platform. The cheering continued. From the elevated position back of the speakers' table, Steve looked down on the crowd. Everybody in the room was standing, clapping, whistling. It seemed difficult for Steve to realize that he was here on this platform. This was the

All-city. He was a part of it. He was Steve Morgan, All-city halfback. Perhaps this was a dream. Perhaps he would wake up and find that the banquet was tomorrow. But Coach Hartford was coming down the line shaking the hand of each player. His handclasp was real.

"Congratulations, Steve," Coach Hartford said.

"Thanks, Coach," Steve replied.

CHAPTER SIXTEEN

STEVE MORGAN was only vaguely conscious of the brilliant flash of news cameras. He had a dim realization that many people were shaking his hand, patting him on the back, but the excitement of the moment made everything hazy in his mind. He looked around for his former old Central teammates—Skiffo Drake, Larry Bowman, Big Bill Toner—but they seemed to be avoiding him. They were standing in a little circle surrounded by a group of admirers. They were laughing and joking, shaking hands. Steve had a feeling that he should be in that circle, but there was no welcoming hand extended to him. He was being shut out by the fellows who had formerly been his best friends. In spite of the fact that Syd Johnson stood by him, Steve felt very much alone.

The banquet was over, and Steve moved toward the door with Syd. They were stopped every few feet by well-wishers, but Steve kept edging toward the lobby. He felt the need for fresh air. He wanted to get away from that exclusive circle of backfield men who had excluded him. He wondered how he would ever be able to play football on the same team with them. A backfield had to work like a unit—a four-man unit. This backfield, it appeared, was going to be a three-man unit. They evidently looked upon Steve Morgan as a spare.

Steve had no desire to play under those circumstances. This moment might have been the high point of his high-school career, but it was rapidly turning to disappointment. What good was the honor of All-city selection if the fellows who shared it with him were not willing to cooperate? They could make him look ridiculous in the state championship game. They could make it appear that he was losing the ball game for Portside. Steve pictured himself being removed from the game, humiliated, disgraced, all because the other members of the *Rambling Rams* had turned against him. It was an unpleasant possibility, and the thought of it left Steve a little sick.

Once out on the sidewalk the fresh air revived him. He turned to Syd Johnson.

"Congratulations, Syd. I was sure you'd make it."

Syd grinned. "Same to you, Steve. Now that the suspense is over, maybe we'd better relax and enjoy the rest of the evening."

"I'd rather go home and go to bed," Steve said. "I feel like a wet mop."

"You'll snap out of it," Syd said. "This ought to be a good dance."

They had crossed the street to the parking garage, and Syd presented the check for his car.

"I hope you remembered to order corsages," Steve said.

"Leave it to me. I think of everything," Syd returned.

"How much do I owe you for the flowers?"

"Two bucks."

"Lucky for you I'm rolling in wealth," Steve said, as he handed Syd the two dollars.

It was almost ten when Syd guided his car into the driveway at Joan Karr's home. Joan lived in a rather pretentious house overlooking the lake, and Steve was impressed by the enormous windows and the landscaped gardens.

"Not bad," Steve said, as they walked up the broad steps. "Papa must be doing all right."

"He owns a couple of lumber mills or something."

Joan met them at the door. "Hello, Syd. Hello, Steve. Won't you come in?"

Steve blinked. Joan looked grownup in her floor-length dress. Her hair-do was something right out of a beauty salon, and wearing high heels she presented quite a different picture from her usual school-girl appearance around the halls of Laurel High.

"Thanks for the flowers, Syd. It was nice of you to send them."

"Nothing at all," Syd said. "They seem to go all right with your dress."

"They're perfect."

Joan was leading them toward the drawing room, and soft music greeted them at the doorway. Standing near the console was Queen Barbara. She wore a long party dress of shimmering blue material, and her honey-colored hair curled in little golden rings about her sun-tanned shoulders. She had a friendly smile and dark, twinkling eyes.

"Barbara," Joan said, "I want you to meet Steve Morgan. Steve, this is Barbara Collins."

Steve had stopped just inside the doorway, slightly confused. It flashed through his mind that Barbara was one of the prettiest girls he had ever seen.

"How do you do," Steve said, regaining some of his composure.

Barbara moved toward him. "Joan has told me a lot about you," she said, extending her hand.

"I hope she hasn't exaggerated."

"I'm sure she hasn't. It's going to be fun going to this dance tonight. I've never attended a dance in the city before."

"I imagine it will be a lot like the dances in Shelton."

"Well, hardly. Shelton is such a small town, you know. We have loads of fun, but it's not the same as in Portside. Take these flowers, for example. They're beautiful, Steve. It was thoughtful of you to send them."

Steve started to color. His collar felt tight, and he darted a quick glance at Syd.

"Oh, Syd and I think of everything," he said, laughing it off.

"Would you like to hear some records?" Joan asked. "I bought a new album this afternoon."

The music was made for dancing, so it was only a matter of moments until some of the smaller rugs were rolled to one side. Steve discovered that Barbara was all that Syd had claimed she was. She was easy to dance with, and before they had played many records she made Steve feel perfectly at ease.

At ten-thirty Joan's parents entered the room, and a round of introductions followed.

"Joan, dear," Mrs. Karr said. "Don't you think it is time to leave for the dance?"

"That might be a good idea." Joan laughed. "We've been having such a good time we almost forgot about it."

The Yacht Club, nestling in park-like grounds near the shore of the lake, was a low, rambling building painted lighthouse white. Rolling lawns stretched from the wide porch to the yacht harbor, and overhead tall poplars swayed in the gentle breeze. Syd drove to the parking area and shut off the motor. Soft music drifted across the tennis courts, and the sound of laughter floated on the night air.

"Let's hurry," Joan said. "It sounds like a grand party."

Steve, caught for a moment in the excitement of the evening, forgot the disappointment he had experienced at the banquet when his former friends had ignored him. As he and Barbara moved up the wide steps and entered the lounge, he actually anticipated a good time. He knew that Barbara would be somewhat of a sensation at the dance. Word would get around that she had been Queen of the Forest Festival, and she had the beauty and the personality to go with her title. It was seldom that a fellow like Steve had the opportunity to accompany a real Festival Queen to a dance. The other boys, he knew, would dart envious glances in his direction, and the girls would either stare in open admiration or gaze upon her with critical eyes. Steve was not worried about their reaction, but he was interested. He couldn't suppress the strange satisfaction that seemed to stir within him. What would Penny Carson think? Penny had turned him down when he had asked for a date. What kind of reception would she give Queen Barbara?

The main ballroom was crowded, and when the girls had returned from the powder room Syd and Steve guided them to the dance floor. The orchestra was playing a current swing tune. Steve and Barbara danced as naturally as they had in the drawing room at Joan's home.

"Oh, it's wonderful," Barbara said, as they glided across the floor. "The music . . . it's simply super, and the decorations . . . I've never seen so much color."

The banners of the eight Portside schools hung from the mezzanine railing that surrounded three sides of the ballroom, and long streamers in the school colors were arched from the banners to the crystal chandelier in the center of the large room.

"That's *my* school over there," Steve said, indicating the crimson and silver of Laurel High.

Suddenly Steve was conscious that he had stressed the

word "my." He was also aware of the note of pride in his voice. It was seldom that he had spoken of Laurel High in such a possessive manner, but the word had slipped out. Well, it was *his* school. He was glad that he felt like claiming it, and he felt a debt of loyalty to the students who had accepted him. He had tried to repay Laurel by wearing the colors of the school in a worthy manner, and now it *was* his school. It would *always* be his school.

There were greetings from many of the dancers on the floor, and several of the fellows grinned at Steve and offered congratulations.

Barbara drew back from Steve and looked at him.

"What dark secret are you hiding from me?" she asked.

"I'm sure I don't know," Steve replied.

"These congratulations . . . what have you done that deserves all this praise?"

"Oh, that," Steve said. "Syd and I were picked for the All-city team. I guess that's the reason."

"And you were going to keep that from me?"

"Not intentionally. I just didn't think you would be interested."

"Does Joan know about this?"

"I imagine she does by now."

Joan and Syd were dancing in the center of the room, and without seeming to do so Barbara guided Steve's steps in their direction. When they were alongside, they heard Joan say, "Why didn't you tell me, Syd?"

Syd replied, "I thought you'd rather find out the hard way."

Barbara looked at Joan. "Why didn't you warn me?" She laughed. "Here we are practically stepping out with the All-city team, and I have to learn it at the dance."

"Syd never tells me anything," Joan said. "He's worse than the Sphinx."

When the orchestra stopped, Steve was surprised at the number of boys who came up to request a dance with Barbara. As her program was practically blank, he could accommodate most of them, but he saved several dances for himself. He had no intention of letting his friends monopolize Queen Barbara.

When he was dancing with other girls he had a chance to observe Barbara from a distance. She was always friendly, full of fun, and her dancing partners seemed to enjoy her company. He even noticed Skiffo Drake and Larry Bowman looking at her from time to time, but neither of them requested a dance.

It was during the third dance that he saw Penny Carson. She was dancing with Don Erickson, from Hilltop High, and she smiled and said "Hello" as they danced past.

Steve grinned back and mumbled a rather belated answer. Penny Carson had spoken to him. It was the first time since the old days at Central High that she had paid any attention to him. He wondered if it was because he had brought Barbara to the dance, or because she felt sorry for him. Whatever it was, it brought a strange glow to Steve.

The tenth dance on the program was a special All-city dance. Only members of the Honor Team were allowed to dance this number, and all of the other couples were expected to watch from the sidelines.

The floor seemed deserted with only eleven couples dancing, but Steve and Barbara were among the chosen few. Steve had a feeling of pride as they moved about the floor, and he was sure from Barbara's manner that she enjoyed this special attention. It was almost as if they were on a stage, and Steve knew that most of the couples standing about the ballroom were watching him and his pretty partner.

Penny Carson was among the onlookers. She had come with a former Central High student who was not a football player. Looking over Barbara's shoulder, Steve's eyes met Penny's, and Penny turned away quickly.

For a moment Steve's mind was not on his dancing. He missed a step and Barbara looked at him in surprise.

"I'm sorry," Steve said. "Guess I got off the beam."

"It was my fault," Barbara said, trying to be nice.

"Don't be silly. I'm to blame. I'll try to keep my mind on my business."

But Steve's mind was not on the business of dancing. He was thinking of Penny Carson, and the embarrassment she had shown when their eyes met. He was thinking of the stolen trophy and of all the trouble it had caused him. He was thinking of the *Rambling Rams* from old Central, and of how each of them had made the All-city while playing for another school. There was something ironic in that. Four backfield men from old Central on the All-city. They could never have made it had they been playing on the same team, but when they were representing different schools each had been outstanding enough to win a place. That had never happened before in Portside, and it would probably never happen again.

Steve was thinking of these things when he collided with Big Bill Toner. The jolt almost knocked him off balance, but he recovered sufficiently to continue dancing.

"I'm sorry, Bill," he said, apologetically.

Big Bill simply glared at him, and guided his partner in another direction.

Steve knew that his face was flushed.

"I guess we should have sat this dance out," he said to Barbara. "I don't know what's the matter with me. I can't seem to make my clumsy feet work right."

"Don't worry about it," Barbara said. "But next time choose a smaller man if you're going to bump into him. From the way that fellow looked at you he could have chewed your head off. What does he have against you?"

"That's a long story," Steve said, trying to laugh it off. "Some day when you have a lot of time I'll tell you about it."

CHAPTER SEVENTEEN

COACH HARTFORD called for a practice session of the All-city team at the Civic Field on Monday afternoon. Twenty-two players reported. This squad was composed of the boys who had made both the first and second teams. They were issued new uniforms that had been purchased by the Portside Chamber of Commerce. The jerseys were bright blue, with a row of gold stars across the chest and large gold numerals on the back. The pants were of gold sateen, and the helmets of blue plastic.

"Pretty flashy," Syd said, as he walked out of the dressing room with Steve.

"I hope we live up to the uniforms," Steve said. "I think I could play better in my old Laurel High outfit."

"We'll get used to them."

The players who had reported early were out on the turf, kicking and passing the new footballs.

Steve spotted Skiffo Drake and Larry Bowman. He wanted to go over and join them, but he knew that such a move would not be well received. If there was ever to be friendship between Steve and the *Rambling Rams* the initiative would have to come from the other players.

Steve and Syd found a ball and started passing it back and forth.

When all of the players were on the field, Coach Hartford and his assistant, Pete Slade, arrived. Hartford blew a whistle and motioned to the squad to gather around.

"We have just two weeks to whip this team in shape," he said. "That means a lot of hard work. I know most of you fellows are in condition because I've seen you play, but now that you've made the All-city there might be a little tendency to let down. I want to start off with a warning. So far as you fellows are concerned, training rules are still in force. That means good food, plenty of sleep, and no smoking. You'll have to lay off dances, evening shows, and other things that will take your mind off the job we have ahead. I'm expecting a lot from you men. If the other coaches in the city didn't think that you could carry through on this assignment you would never have been selected for this team. If you have what it takes you'll do all right. If you haven't, well, that's your funeral. It's up to you. I want all of you in bed by ten o'clock every night. I want you to report for practice on time, and I want you to work while you're here. If any of you can't agree wholeheartedly to this program, you can turn in your suit right now. If you keep your suit I'll take that as your assurance that you're ready and willing to do everything I say to win this game."

Coach Hartford paused, and looked slowly around the circle of players. No one made a move to turn in his suit.

"Good. That must mean that you're ready to go to work. Now some of my ideas may not jibe with what your regular coaches have taught you, but fundamentally the game of football is always the same. Coaches differ only in minor details. Here are some of the things every coach wants. He wants a team that can tackle, block, and run with the ball. He wants a backfield that can pass and kick, and pound the line for steady gains. He wants a line that can open holes on offense, and close them up on defense. He wants fast, alert players who can keep their eyes on the ball, and their minds on the game. He wants weight and speed, brains and brawn. Now I don't know how well you fellows measure up to those requirements, but we're going to find out."

Coach Hartford handed Pete Slade a clip board with the names of the second-team players.

"If you'll take this squad down to the west end of the field, and run through some simple formations, I'll get started with this first team."

When the second team had moved away, Hartford turned to his squad.

"Take the positions that were assigned to you on the All-city team."

The line formed, and Steve moved into the backfield with Skiffo Drake, Larry Bowman, and Big Bill Toner. Not a word was exchanged between them. They stood with their hands on their hips, awaiting Coach Hartford's directions.

Orin Wagner, the center, was crouching over the ball. Coach Hartford stood in front of him and grinned at his backfield.

"I never thought I'd see you fellows in the same backfield again. You did all right when you were playing for Central High, and there's no reason why you shouldn't do all right here."

Steve winced. He could think of a reason why they might not do all right, and he was pretty sure that Coach Hartford sensed there might be friction in this backfield.

"If you fellows are ever going to win the state championship," the coach said, "you'll have to work together. You'll have to forget everything that has happened in the past. You'll have to forget that you played for Wallingford, and Hilltop, and Laurel—even old Central. This team doesn't represent any of those schools. This team represents a city. If you've ever had any personal differences you'll have to rub them out for the good of Portside. If you can't do that, you don't belong on this team."

Steve glanced quickly at the other *Rambling Rams*. They were staring straight ahead, like statues, and from all appearances the coach's words were having little effect on them. If only they would break down, declare a truce, Steve would have given anything to show them that he could forget the differences of the past. But there was no evidence of a change in their attitude. They resented Steve's presence in this backfield. Their expressions showed plainly how they felt.

Coach Hartford started them off with four plays that worked from a "T" formation. Because these players were the pick of the city football teams, they were quick to learn. Within an hour he had increased the number of plays to eight.

Larry Bowman called the signals from his position at quarterback. Skiffo Drake and Big Bill Toner ran through the plays like automatons. When Steve Morgan carried the ball they formed interference for him because the play called for it, and not because of any personal desire to do so. There was no conversation between them. There were several times when Steve wanted to

offer encouragement or ask advice, but because the other members of the backfield were shunning him he knew that it would not be wise to break the ice. The situation was not right, but Steve could do nothing about it. He made up his mind to play as well as he could, and to hope that the tension would break before the big game with the All-state team.

When Coach Hartford called his players together on the second night of practice, he announced the names of the men who had been selected for the All-state team.

"You fellows are in for a rugged time in that championship game," he said. "The All-state backfield is about as nice a combination as a coach could want. Earl Nevers, from Everett, will play left half. They've turned out some pretty good ball players in Everett, and Earl Nevers is among the best of them. He's big, fast, and plenty tough. Bob Reed, from Lewis and Clark High, Spokane, is going to play quarterback. Bob does the hundred in a shade under ten, and if he ever gets loose he'll give you fellows a merry chase. Butch Hogan, who played fullback from Bremerton in the cross-state league, has been chosen for that spot on the All-state. Butch weighs one hundred and ninety, and he's a powerhouse on offense. When he hits the line something has to crack, and it generally isn't Butch. He's a trouble-maker, and if you can't stop him he's going to smear you all over the landscape. For right half they've picked Stan Williams, from Walla Walla. I don't know much about Williams except that two or three college coaches are

after him. That means he has something on the ball and
you fellows will find out what it is when you meet him
face to face."

Coach Hartford looked at his list.

"The line averages one hundred and eighty-two
pounds. They have an edge on us of about three pounds
to the man. That might mean a lot or it might not. It all
depends on how much fight you fellows can show. Hap
Nelson, of Everett, is playing right end. He's eighteen,
and is six feet four inches tall. You probably saw him in
the state basketball tournament last year. He's that lanky
center who worried the life out of Ravenna High. Right
tackle is Abe Kessler, from Stadium High, Tacoma.
Abe is built like a grizzly bear. Joe Bekins, of Aberdeen,
is right guard. Joe worked in a logging camp last
summer, and he's tougher than a donkey engine. For
center, they have Harry Cowan, from Yakima. Harry is
a cinch for a State College berth next season. Johnny
Gatta, of Hoquiam, plays left guard. They tell me
Johnny tore holes in the Southwest League this season.
Left tackle is Ray Kahn, from the Bellingham *Red
Raiders*. Look out for this boy Kahn. He has a habit of
playing in the opposing team's backfield most of the
time. Then there's Stuart Young, from Wenatchee, in
the left-end spot. He's a swell running mate for Hap

Nelson, of Everett. Those two fellows are going to make the ends pretty hard to circle. Well, there you have it, gang. If you can beat this crowd you're the state champions. But it isn't going to be a picnic. It's going to be the toughest football game you ever played."

The practice session that night lasted until six o'clock. They had to turn the field lights on at four-thirty, and for an hour and a half they drilled under artificial lights. Coach Hartford really started cracking the whip that second night. He was all over the place, shouting instructions, bawling warnings, teaching new plays, offering advice.

"Get that ball up into your armpit, Drake, and keep your head down. You carry the ball like a suitcase. Toner, how many times have I told you to get moving on that twenty-two play? Do I have to get in there and lead you by the hand? Erickson, if you're going to box that end in, smash into him. You can't push him around with your finger-tips. Wagner, spread your legs wider when you center the ball. Dig your cleats in and drive ahead. If you don't you'll end up sitting down in the backfield."

There were times during that first week of practice when the Portside team looked pretty good, but there were other times when Coach Hartford was ready to tear his hair out.

"I ought to resign. I ought to walk out of here and leave you fellows cold. You're supposed to be the best football material that Portside can offer. Do you know what you look like? You look like some team from the sticks—some ham outfit from a third-rate league. Eleven trained apes could do a better job than you're doing."

For a time the team would settle down and look like championship material. Then Coach Hartford would grin.

"Now you're rolling. I can see a faint ray of hope for you. If you'd play like that all of the time you'd be sitting on top of the world."

It was a hectic week. When the long practice sessions were over, the tired players would drag their way into the showers and then head for home. For Steve Morgan the days followed one another in a routine pattern—breakfast, school, football practice, dinner, study, bed. At ten sharp he was under the covers, and at ten-five he was sound asleep.

By the middle of the second week Coach Hartford began to slack off on his training sessions. The last scrimmage was held on Wednesday.

There had been times during the practice period when it had been necessary for members of the backfield to talk with one another, but whenever the other three directed their remarks to Steve Morgan, the conversa-

tion was limited to essentials. Occasionally there was criticism in their tone, but Steve Morgan was resigned to that.

"Play wider on that twenty-eight play," Skiffo Drake said. "Do you want Big Bill to knock you for a loop?"

"Okay," Steve said. "I'll play wider."

There were tense moments when Steve might have made something of their remarks, but rather than stir up antagonism he elected to remain silent. He had hoped that after two weeks of practice there might be some change in the attitude of the other backfield men, but as the time for the big game drew near he could see nothing that indicated any feeling of friendship toward him. Skiffo Drake sneered openly whenever Steve made a mistake. Big Bill Toner, his thick jaw set, and his eyes on the ground, paid no attention to the Portside left half. Larry Bowman shared Skiffo's disgust, but once or twice Larry looked at Steve questioningly, as if he were not sure of the feelings that his expression registered.

Steve had been so busy with his school work and his football practice that he found little time to talk to Yogi Zimmerman. Frequently he saw the little freshman scurrying about the halls with a worried look on his face. Yogi always seemed to be in a hurry, so Steve made no effort to stop him.

On Friday morning, the day before the big game, Yogi was waiting at Steve's locker. Yogi had a big grin on his face, and there was a new sparkle in his eyes.

"What are you so happy about?" Steve asked, his tone a bit surly.

"Everything is going to be all right, Steve," Yogi said. "I've cracked the case of the missing trophy."

"You have?" Steve gripped Yogi by the shoulders. "Tell me about it. Who has the trophy?"

"Not so fast," Yogi said. "I can't tell you about it yet."

"Why not?"

"I've never let you down, have I, Steve?"

"No."

"Okay, then. You'll have to take my word for it. The mystery has been solved. I've been working on it all week."

"But when will the trophy be returned?" Steve asked.

"By Saturday, I hope."

" '*I hope*'? What do you mean by that?"

"To tell you the truth, Steve, I'm not absolutely sure. Something might go wrong. But if my plan works, the trophy will show up. If it doesn't, I hate to think of the mess that will be stirred up in the newspapers."

"What have the newspapers to do with it?" Steve demanded.

"Nothing, yet. We'll just have to sit tight, and pray that my plan works."

Steve plied Yogi with other questions, but he could get no more information from him. Finally he gave up.

Steve spent a restless day. Yogi's words kept going over and over in his mind, and he searched them for some clue to the mystery. He could find no explanation.

"If that freckled freshman is kidding me along," Steve muttered, "I'll . . . I'll . . . " He could think of no punishment dire enough for such a development.

Steve ate dinner in silence that evening, and then went to his room to rest. He stretched out on his bed and stared at the ceiling. If Yogi had really solved the case of the missing trophy it might make the difference between winning and losing the game on the following day. He felt sure that if a satisfactory explanation could be given, and if his name could be cleared of all blame, Skiffo Drake, Larry Bowman, and Big Bill Toner would realize that they had made a terrible mistake. If only Yogi was right! Steve opened and closed his fists. The palms of his hands were moist. He felt nervous. This was no way to feel the night before the big game. He should be relaxed, at ease.

He heard the telephone ringing and finally his mother's voice calling from the foot of the stairs.

"It's for you, Steve."

Steve put his feet on the floor and straightened his tie. "Who is it?" he mumbled as he brushed through the dining room on the way to the phone.

"I don't know, Steve. Some girl."

"Some girl?" Steve hesitated. "Maybe I'm not in. Maybe I just stepped out."

"Maybe you'll march out and answer the phone like a gentleman," his mother said.

Steve went to the kitchen and picked up the waiting receiver.

"Hello," he said, experimentally.

"Hello, Steve," the girl said. "This is Penny Carson."

"Oh . . . uh . . . hello, Penny," Steve gulped.

"Are you going to the Tolo Dance tomorrow night to celebrate the championship game?"

"Why . . . uh . . . . no, Penny. I guess not. Haven't thought much about it. Been pretty busy."

"Would you like to go with me, Steve? You know this is the one dance during the year when the girls are supposed to ask the boys."

"Yeah . . . I know. Why . . . uh . . . sure, Penny. That is, if you really want me to."

"Dad said we can have the car. The dance starts at nine-thirty. Can you come over about nine?"

"Okay, Penny. But tell me . . . why the sudden change?"

"Hasn't Yogi told you . . . about the trophy, I mean?"

"Yogi? Are you in cahoots with that little monkey?"

"Yogi and I are great pals," Penny said.

"And you know something about the trophy?"

"Yogi said he would tell you, but if he hasn't it will have to wait. See you tomorrow night, Steve."

"Tomorrow night, yeah."

"I hope you win the game."

"Thanks a lot, Penny."

STATE CHAMPIONSHIP GAME

THE LINE-UP

ALL-CITY		ALL-STATE
Don Erickson Hilltop	LER	Hap Nelson Everett
Jim Eaton Hilltop	LTR	Abe Kessler Stadium
Brad Peeler Ravenna	LGR	Joe Bekins Aberdeen
Orin Wagner Airport	C	Harry Cowan Yakima
Syd Johnson Laurel	RGL	Johnny Gatta Hoquiam
Tad Brownlee Forest	RTL	Ray Kahn Bellingham
Chuck Mallet Mercer	REL	Stuart Young Wenatchee
Skiffo Drake Ravenna	RHL	Earl Nevers Everett
Larry Bowman Hilltop	Q	Bob Reed Lewis and Clark
Big Bill Toner Wallingford	F	Butch Hogan Bremerton
Steve Morgan Laurel	LHR	Stan Williams Walla Walla

THE ALARM clock rang in Steve's room at seven o'clock on Saturday morning. He had set it for the usual time, as he wanted nothing to interfere with the routine he had followed for the past two weeks. It was a temptation to sleep late on a morning like this, but Steve knew that irregular hours might have a bad effect upon his playing.

While his mother was preparing breakfast, Steve scanned the sports pages of the morning paper. There was plenty of space devoted to the game, with pictures of both the All-city and All-state teams, but there was no mention of the stolen trophy. Steve had hoped that the papers would carry the story, for Yogi had hinted at that possibility. When he found nothing to clear up the situation, he was disappointed. Perhaps Yogi's plan had failed. Perhaps Yogi's dream of solving the mystery had been a dream, and nothing more. But there must have been something to Yogi's story, or Penny Carson would never have called.

Steve ate a breakfast of soft boiled eggs, toast, and cocoa.

"You looked worried, Steve," his mother said, as she served the food.

"I guess I am worried," Steve admitted. "Things have been breaking a little too fast for me."

"I'll be glad when this football is over," his mother said. "Maybe you can get some rest."

Steve spent part of the morning repairing a broken goose neck on his bicycle. He seldom rode his bicycle any more, but the job kept his hands busy and his mind occupied. At eleven o'clock Syd Johnson called.

"How you makin' out, Steve?" he asked.

"I'm all right," Steve said. "Little jittery is all."

"It won't be long now. How about picking you up at twelve-thirty? Coach wants us at the stadium by one o'clock."

"Okay. Thanks."

Because it was Thanksgiving Day, Steve's father had not gone to the office. Steve had secured tickets on the fifty-yard line for his family.

"Be seeing you after the game," he shouted, when Syd sounded the horn in front of the house.

"You be careful, Steve," his mother called after him. "I don't know what I'd do if you were hurt."

"Not a chance," Steve called back.

The crowd was already arriving at the University Stadium when Syd pulled up back of the Field House and parked in the area reserved for coaches and players.

Several players were already getting into their uniforms when Steve and Syd entered the dressing room. Pete Slade was checking the players off as they arrived.

"Suit up," he said, "and Syd, you'd better have that ankle taped."

Big Bill Toner was adjusting Skiffo Drake's shoulder pad for him. There was no sign of recognition from them as Steve slumped down on the bench and started to unlace his shoes. Steve had a premonition of trouble ahead. He wondered if Yogi had made up that story about the stolen trophy just to give him encouragement. Yogi had said the trophy would be returned by Saturday. Well, here it was Saturday, and there was no sign of the missing cup. Steve felt blue. He knew that his presence in the backfield would only lead to friction, and with the three other backfield men against him the odds were pretty one-sided. He thought of going to Coach Hartford and asking him to put a substitute in his position at left half. He wondered how the coach would receive such a suggestion. Hartford might think he was yellow. That would never do. He decided that he would have to stay on the job and let the breaks of the game determine his lot.

The squad was dressed by one-thirty, and Coach Hartford called them to attention.

"You're going out on the field for a twenty-minute warm-up," he said. "Pass the ball around, and I want you kickers to get off a few punts. Ends are to practice going down on kicks. You linemen, get your arms and legs limbered up. When I give the signal you're coming back here for final instructions."

The players filed out of the dressing room and started down the long tunnel that led to the field. Their cleats clattered on the cement floor and sent hollow echoes bounding ahead of them in the narrow passageway. A circle of sunshine marked the end of the tunnel, and the Portside All-city trotted out on the field, their blue jerseys and gold pants offering a pleasing contrast to the green turf. A cheer started in the stands, growing in volume. The stadium was more than half filled, and the crowd was still coming. Steve had witnessed many a Pacific Coast Conference game on this field, but he had never played in the University Stadium before. The size of the big horseshoe left him a little breathless, but he knew that once the game had started he could forget the crowd and concentrate on football.

The first team lined up and ran through a few signals as they moved down the field. When they reached the far end they broke up and started kicking and passing as the coach had requested.

Steve took his place with Skiffo, Larry, and Big Bill Toner. There was no talk between them. They went through the motions like so many deaf mutes. It struck Steve that this was silly, but there was nothing he could do about it. When Skiffo kicked a nice sixty-yard punt, Steve wanted to say, "Nice going," but he thought better of it. Skiffo would probably take it the wrong way. Steve sensed that the tension in this backfield had almost reached the snapping point, and he had no desire to start the fireworks. Perhaps they could play together without being friends. The first quarter would determine that. There had been times in practice when they had worked smoothly in spite of their differences. With a little competition they might do all right.

Another cheer from the stands announced the arrival of the All-state team. They wore red jerseys and gray helmets, and they trotted out on the field with all the assurance of a college squad. They looked big, and confident, and ready for action.

"Take a gander at that Johnny Gatta," Syd Johnson said, as he sidled up to Steve. "He's bigger than a moose."

"You can outsmart a moose," Steve said with a grin.

"Yeah, but I can't outpush one. He's liable to plant a number twelve hoof in the middle of my back."

"That whole line looks plenty tough."

"We'll have to go over them or under them. I don't think we'll ever get through them."

Coach Hartford was signaling to his men, and the Portside team started back up the tunnel to the dressing room. They sprawled on the benches between the lockers, and Coach Hartford sat on a small table near the shower-room door and looked his players over.

"This is it, gang," he said. "I'm not going to give you a song and dance about breaking your necks for dear old Portside. All I'm asking you to do is play football. Smart, heads-up football. This All-state team is big and fast, and if you aren't on your toes every minute they'll make monkeys out of you. But they aren't supermen. They pull their football pants on the same way you do, and I imagine they can make mistakes like any other eleven players. Your job is to beat them to the punch—keep a couple of jumps ahead of them."

Coach Hartford looked down the line. "Where's Drake?"

"Here, Coach," Skiffo said, lifting his hand.

"I don't want you to open up much in the first quarter.

I'm appointing you captain for this game, and that means I'm putting a lot of confidence in you. If I send a player in with instructions you are to follow them implicitly. Otherwise, you're on your own. During this quarter I want you to feel out the other team—look for the weak spots. Hold off on the passes until you find out if you can make yardage without them. And listen, Drake—during the first quarter I want you to kick on the third down. If I change my mind I'll send word to you. If you win the toss I want you to defend the east goal."

Hartford looked at his watch.

"Erickson and Mallet," he said, "I want you to keep on your feet when they're coming around your end. Turn those plays in. If Bob Reed or Earl Nevers ever get outside of you they'll make a track meet out of it. Understand? Smear the interference and turn those plays in. Let the tackles and the secondary worry about stopping the ball carrier. And another thing, I'm going to be watching you on punts. A lot of ball games have been lost because the ends didn't get down on punts."

"Three minutes, Coach," Pete Slade said.

"Okay, gang! More power to you. Let's see you take this game."

The players shuffled to their feet and started for the tunnel. As they moved down the passageway for the second time, Steve's mind was a jumble of thoughts. Yogi Zimmerman had failed him. Here it was game time, and the missing trophy had not appeared. Skiffo Drake, Larry Bowman, and Big Bill Toner were still as antagonistic as ever. The All-city backfield was split wide open, and anything could happen.

Steve wondered about Penny Carson. Why had she asked him to the dance? She must have known that Yogi's story about the trophy was just the product of a wild imagination. Yogi was only a freshman—a little kid, living in a dream world. His interest in Steve was the result of hero worship, and his talk about finding the missing trophy was an effort to be a "big shot" in Steve's eyes. There were lots of freshmen like Yogi Zimmerman, trying to show off, trying to make an impression. Yogi would grow out of it one of these days. Steve felt that he had encouraged Yogi too much. He should never have taken the freshman so seriously.

The large stadium was filled to capacity when the Portside team made its second appearance. Students from all eight Portside high schools were assembled on the north side of the field. They made a colorful display with pom-poms, banners, and rooting caps. A one-hundred-piece band composed of the best high-school players in the city was just leaving the field after a marching demonstration. Eight yell kings, wearing their respective school colors, were dancing around in front of the Portside stands, leading the cheers, encouraging the applause. It was an enthusiastic ovation, and in spite of his troubled mind Steve was thrilled as he trotted out on the green turf.

While the All-city and All-state teams waited in front of their respective benches, the two captains met with the officials in the center of the field. A silver coin spun in the sunlight, and the referee bent down to determine the flip. When he straightened up, Skiffo Drake was pointing to the east end of the field. That meant Portside had won the toss. Skiffo had elected to defend the east goal. The State team chose to receive.

Steve fitted a helmet over his head and adjusted the strap. Then he joined the Portside players in a brief huddle. Eleven men locked hands in a little ritual that was meant to tie them together for one purpose—the winning of this game. But to the four backfield men that handclasp was not as impressive as it should have been. To Steve, it lacked sincerity, for he knew that three of these players nursed a grudge against him. To Larry Bowman, Skiffo Drake, and Big Bill Toner, it was only a formality. To these three it might have meant something had not Steve Morgan been in the backfield, but Steve spoiled the charm. It was just a handclasp, nothing more.

The members of the Portside team took their positions on the forty-yard line. Big Bill Toner had been chosen to kick off, and he stood a few yards back of the line, waiting for the referee's whistle. Skiffo Drake was at Big Bill's right, ready to drop back into safety position after the kick.

"Ready, Portside?" the referee called.

Skiffo raised his hand.

"Ready, State?"

Bob Reed, captain of the All-state team, waved his arm to indicate his team was ready.

The referee's whistle sounded.

Big Bill Toner moved forward, gathering speed. The toe of his shoe collided with the ball, and the pigskin lifted over the heads of the State players, sailing end over end far down the field.

Earl Nevers took it on the five, and started up the field, behind rapidly forming interference. A State tackle crashed into Steve on the fifty-yard line, but Steve shook him off and regained his feet. He moved in on Nevers, but Larry Bowman beat him to the tackle.

Nevers was down on the thirty-five. He had returned the kick thirty yards.

The State team went into a huddle, and when they trotted to their positions they looked ready for business, formidable. Stan Williams, the Walla Walla flash, took the ball from Reed and started around left end, but Chuck Mallet began spilling the interference and Williams had to cut back. Larry Bowman moved in fast from the secondary and caught him coming off tackle. The play netted four yards.

It was second down, six to go.

This time Butch Hogan hit the center of the line like a battering ram, and he picked up five yards with brute force.

It was third down, one yard to go.

Bob Reed punched it over in a quarterback sneak that put the ball on the fifty-yard line.

Skiffo Drake called for time out. There was no sense in letting this team get rolling so early in the game.

Portside went into a huddle.

"Wagner," Skiffo said, "you and Johnson and Peeler have to figure a way to stop Butch Hogan. If he starts blasting through the center, we're sunk. Get under him. Close that line up."

Skiffo's little talk must have done some good, for the

next play was Hogan over center. This time he hit a stone wall. It was second down, ten to go.

"Look out for a pass," Skiffo shouted, but he called the play wrong. It was Earl Nevers off tackle, and the ball was down on Portside's forty-four-yard line. Nevers made six yards on the play.

Butch Hogan dropped back in a kick formation, and Skiffo, playing safety, moved back. But Butch didn't kick. He ran to the right and threw a pass to Hap Nelson who took it on the thirty. Larry Bowman brought him down on the twenty-six.

The next four plays were line smashes that were good for three and four yards at a clip. The first thing Portside knew, State had the ball on the ten-yard line, and it was first down.

Skiffo called for another "time out." Anything to stop this relentless march. But State was not to be stopped. When the referee signaled to play ball, Butch Hogan picked up five off right tackle, and State was set for a touchdown.

The Portside stands were unusually quiet, while an improvised rooting section on the south side of the field was cheering wildly for State.

The Portside secondary was bunched in behind the line now. The State team came out of the huddle. The men were grinning confidently. They packed power, and every man on the team knew it.

Bob Reed crouched behind the State center, surveying the Portside backfield. He started calling the shift.

"One . . . two . . . three . . . hip!"

The ball was snapped. Reed spun around, faked it to Nevers. The rest of the State backfield was moving right. Reed sent a shovel pass to Stan Williams, who was running for the left sidelines. Eaton, Portside left tackle, was off his feet. He made a grab for Stan's legs, but missed. Interference boxed Don Erickson out of the play. Ten yards from the sideline, Stan cut sharply. He collided with Steve Morgan at the goal line, but the ball was over. State had scored.

Steve Morgan got to his feet slowly. Skiffo Drake was standing nearby, hands on his hips. He glared at Steve.

"Nice going, Morgan. You sure smeared him on that play."

Steve caught the sarcasm in Skiffo's words, but he controlled his temper. He could have asked Skiffo where *he* was on the play. He could have asked what happened to Erickson and Eaton, but he held his tongue. It would sound like an alibi.

The Portside team lined up on the three-yard line.

The State drive had taken the sap out of them. Butch Hogan kicked the goal. The scoreboard recorded in bold numerals: STATE 7, PORTSIDE 0.

When the two teams were ready to resume play, State was in kicking position and Portside was spread out over the east end of the field ready to receive.

The ball came low and fast. It bounced against Larry Bowman's chest and slithered off at a crazy angle. Larry had only enough time to fall on the ball, for the State end was down on him. The referee put it in play on the thirty-two-yard line, and Portside went into a huddle.

"Number twenty-two," Skiffo Drake said. That was an off-tackle smash, with Big Bill Toner packing the ball.

The Portside team moved to their positions. On this play Steve was supposed to take the end out. Skiffo called for the shift. The ball was snapped.

Steve spotted his man, rolled into him, but the end put powerful hands on Steve's shoulders and shoved him into the turf. Then he leaped over Steve's twisting body and smeared the play at the line of scrimmage.

Back in the huddle, Drake looked at Steve.

"Thought you were supposed to get that end."

"I'll get him next time," Steve promised.

Skiffo grunted in disgust. "Number thirty-two," he snapped.

That was the same play off the other tackle. This time it was good for two yards. Bowman got the end, but the secondary was in there plugging the hole.

The ball was on the thirty-four-yard line, and it was third down coming up.

Skiffo called for punt formation. The ends moved out, and Big Bill Toner dropped back for the kick.

He got it away, a long, high punt that dropped into the arms of Bob Reed on the State twenty-two-yard line. Both Erickson and Chuck Mallet were down on him, and they nailed him on the twenty-five.

Steve glanced at the scoreboard at the east end of the stadium. There were five minutes left in the quarter. He wondered if State could engineer another sustained drive. It began to look as if they could, for it took only four plays for them to put the ball on the mid-field stripe. Bob Reed was good for fifteen of those yards. He made it by skirting Chuck Mallet's end. Reed was all Coach Hartford had said he was. He was as fast as a lightning bolt and as hard to catch.

When they had crossed the forty-yard marker, State started passing. One pass was incomplete, but the second one clicked for a twelve-yard gain. They ran the ends a couple of times, and then they tried a long pass toward the southeast corner of the field. Skiffo sensed it coming, and he was there to intercept it. He streaked down the sideline for fifteen yards before he was forced out of bounds.

It was Portside's ball on the thirty-yard stripe. This time Steve could not restrain the impulse to congratulate Skiffo.

"Nice going, Skiffo," he said, as they walked back to the huddle.

"Save your breath," Skiffo snapped.

In the huddle Skiffo looked at Steve. "Think you can pack the ball without fumbling?"

Steve's eyes narrowed. If Skiffo was going to force the issue, that was all right with him. He had taken about all he could from these fellows.

"You're running the team," Steve said. "Make up your own mind."

The linemen looked up, surprised at Steve's tone.

"Okay," Skiffo said, "if you're going to get smart about it, here's your chance. Number twenty-six."

Number twenty-six was a play around right end, with Steve carrying the ball. As he crouched down for the shift Steve could feel the anger churning within him. He took the ball from Skiffo and started right. Hap Nelson was shoving his interference around, so Steve cut in. He found a hole off tackle. Stan Williams, the State right half, made a dive for him, but Steve spun around and

The second pass clicked for a twelve-yard gain

broke loose. He crossed the forty, the forty-five, the forty-seven before Butch Hogan hit him. He was down on the forty-eight.

A cheer went up from the north stands. Steve Morgan had made eighteen yards on one play. The linesmen were moving the chain. It was first down, ten to go.

Back in the huddle Skiffo Drake said, "Who told you to cut in on that play?"

"Nobody," Steve answered. "I just figured it out myself."

"After this follow your interference."

"Listen," Steve said. "You play it your way; I'll play it mine."

"Lay off, you guys," someone growled. "We'll get penalized."

"Number twenty-two," Skiffo said.

Big Bill Toner piled up on the fifty-yard line. It was second down coming up, eight to go.

Larry Bowman took the ball on the next play. The State line decided that he was all through. The ball was still on the fifty-yard line when the whistle sounded, and it was third down.

"Punt formation," Skiffo said.

Big Bill's kick bounced out of bounds on the twelve-yard marker.

With three minutes left in the quarter, State started another long march. They had reached the forty-yard line when the gun sounded, ending the first period.

While the teams were changing goals the water boys were out on the field with cool water and damp towels. Steve took off his helmet and rubbed his face and the back of his neck.

When play was resumed, it was third down and one yard to go for State. Hogan punched it over for six yards, putting the ball on the forty-six. Then Earl Nevers faded for a long pass, and Hap Nelson took it on the thirty and ran it down to the twenty before Larry Bowman snagged him.

This State team had a powerful drive. Four yards, six yards, eight yards! They were down in pay dirt. Two yards to go for a touchdown.

Steve was backing up the Portside line when Skiffo came along and gave him a shove.

"Get in closer," he barked. "No use stopping him back of the goal line."

"How about you saving this game?" Steve retorted. "You're doing most of the talking."

Syd Johnson straightened up in the line and turned around.

"Cut it out," he snapped. "This is no time for that kind of stuff."

The State team was coming out of the huddle. Butch Hogan got the ball. He hit the line like a buzz bomb and took everything along with him. The referee's arms went into the air. State had scored again.

This time Butch's try-for-point failed, and the scoreboard read: STATE 13, PORTSIDE 0.

That was not the way it should be. Steve knew it, and he was shaking his head as he walked back to his position to receive. Skiffo and Big Bill Toner were engaged in a little argument on the twenty-yard line. Steve could not hear what they were saying, but he could tell by their expressions that there was disagreement. Larry Bowman moved over toward them, and Steve could hear Larry saying:

"Come on, you lugs. That kind of talk won't get you anywhere. How about playin' a little football?"

Big Bill Toner moved off, and Skiffo planted his feet on the twenty-yard line and glared in Steve's direction. Steve knew that he was the cause of this bickering, and he would have given the world to have it different. If only Coach Hartford would pull him out of the game, maybe the other three could get working together. Steve knew they could play football, but not while they were fighting among themselves. That was evident when Portside got the ball again.

Big Bill Toner got mixed up on a signal and ran off in the wrong direction, leaving Skiffo holding the ball. Skiffo got smacked for a five-yard loss. Larry Bowman collided with Steve on the next play, and it knocked him into Skiffo, who was carrying the ball. Skiffo lost his footing and fell back of the line of scrimmage.

On the next play Big Bill Toner fumbled the ball. Hap Nelson, from Everett, fell on the pigskin, and it was State's ball on the Portside thirty-five.

Skiffo blamed Steve for all of this misfortune, and he was not hesitant about saying so. After the fumble, Skiffo was ready to toss in his helmet and quit. The Portside backfield was cracking up. Even Larry Bowman and Big Bill Toner were crabbing.

Coach Hartford, pacing the sidelines, was aware of what was going on. He could see the results of broken morale. He thought of pulling out the whole backfield and sending in the second string. Then he glanced at the scoreboard. Three minutes were left in the half. He changed his mind and called Bert Logan from the players' bench. He put his arm around Bert's shoulder until State had run one play.

"Take Steve Morgan's place," he said, giving Bert a shove.

Steve Morgan came off the field with his head down, his shoulders hunched. He knew that Coach Hartford had put his finger on the cause of the trouble in the Portside backfield, but he was afraid it was too late. The damage had been done. Steve sought the oblivion of the substitute bench and slumped down.

No one spoke to Steve. That was all right with him. As he rested his head on his hands, he wished that he could crawl into a hole. He had never played such miserable football, and this was the day when he should be reaching the height of his high-school career. He could sense the dejection of the players who shared the bench with him. They had cause for being down-hearted. Their team was making a mess of this game. The last three minutes of the first half did not help raise their spirits.

State completed another long pass that took the ball to the twenty. A short pass put it on the eight, and then Butch Hogan plowed through the center of the Portside line to score the third touchdown. He missed the kick, and the scoreboard announced: STATE 19, PORTSIDE 0.

The timekeeper's gun exploded like a firecracker, and the half was over.

CHAPTER NINETEEN

THE STATE players trotted off the field, grinning in a self-satisfied way. They had played well, and the stands gave them a big hand as they disappeared in the tunnel.

The Portside players came at a walk, and there was nothing but gloom written on their faces. Outplayed at every turn of the game, they had little cause for rejoicing. Even the Portside substitutes looked weary as they trudged along behind the others. Steve Morgan brought up the rear. He felt as if every eye in the immense stadium was on him, and he was not far wrong. There were hundreds who wondered what had happened to Steve Morgan. They had seen him play brilliant ball against Forest High in the city league, but in this game he had made only one run that hinted at his ability. Steve was glad when the tunnel closed in about him. Those eyes were gone—those thousands of eyes staring at him, wondering.

As he moved up the long, dim passageway he was conscious of the odor of perspiration, the clatter of cleats, the heavy breathing of the players ahead of him. No one spoke. They pushed forward like sheep following some bellwether. So this was the great All-city game, the grand moment that had beckoned all through the years to Steve Morgan. How he had hoped that the day would come when he could play in the All-city game. How he had worked, and sweated, and prayed for this day. And now it was here. This was it—bleak, disappointing, discouraging. If he could only run away from it all, disappear. He hated to enter the locker room. He hated to face his teammates. He stopped for a drink at the fountain outside the dressing-room door, stalling for time. When all of the players had entered, there was nothing to do but follow them. Steve pushed on the door.

On the threshold Steve caught his breath. The sight that greeted him sent a vibrant chill tingling through his body. He could feel his heart pounding under his sweat-soaked jersey. The blood was rushing through his veins, pumping into his arms, his legs. He could feel it throbbing in his wrists. He could feel it surging through him like a warm tide.

The room was deathly quiet. Players were slouched on the benches, staring at the little table near the shower-room door. Coach Hartford was standing near the table, a sheet of paper in his hand. And on the table, spotlighted by a finger of sunlight that filtered through a window, was the gleaming silver trophy that had been stolen from Central High.

The All-city Trophy!

Steve's teeth bit into his underlip. It was all he could do to keep the tears of joy from his eyes. He wanted to shout. He wanted to dance. He wanted to sing. But he held himself in check. Quietly, he slipped along the wall and slid onto a bench in a dark corner of the room.

Yogi had not failed him. Yogi had come through with colors flying. He had said the All-city trophy would be returned, and here it was, in all its shimmering brilliance. Good little Yogi!

Coach Hartford broke the stillness of the room.

"Let's have your attention," he said, and there was a little catch in his voice. There was no need for him to worry about attention. Every eye in the room was focused on him.

"I don't know how this trophy got here," he said, "but you'll have to agree that there is no question about its being here. This note was attached to the cup. I think it will explain a number of things. It might even have something to do with this football game we are playing today."

Coach Hartford cleared his throat and started to read:

To Coach Hartford:

We are hereby returning the All-city Cup which was taken from Central High School on the evening of June 10. In explanation we would like to say that this trophy was taken by a group of boys belonging to a social club in one of the Portside high schools. At first we looked upon it as a prank, a sort of souvenir, but we have come to realize the seriousness of the offense, as others who were not responsible have been charged with its theft. Please accept our apologies, and our assurance that nothing like this will happen again.

"The note is unsigned," Coach Hartford said, "but that is not important. The cup is back, and if I'm not wrong it should clear up some ugly charges that have been floating around. Anybody here want to say anything?"

There was a moment of silence as the players looked at one another. Finally, Skiffo Drake shuffled to his feet.

"I don't know just how to say this, Coach, but I figure I owe Steve Morgan a public apology. I thought all along that he stole that trophy, and now I realize how wrong

I was. I've been an awful sap, and I wouldn't blame Steve if he never forgave me. All I can say is that if there's any way I can make up to him for all the harm I've done him I'll be more than glad to do it."

Larry Bowman was the next man on his feet.

"I feel like a heel," he said. "I've been guilty of helping to spread the rumor that Steve swiped that cup. It just goes to show how a fellow can take an awful beating for something he never did. I've been doing a lot of thinking the last few minutes, and it seems as though there isn't any way I can square myself, but like Skiffo, I'm going to try."

When Larry Bowman sat down, Big Bill Toner stood up.

"I'm sorry I ever suspected Steve. I should have known a fellow like him wouldn't steal that cup. I mean it when I say I'm sorry, and I hope Steve will forgive me."

Coach Hartford looked around the room.

"Where's Steve Morgan?" he asked.

Somebody motioned to the secluded corner where Steve sat hunched with his head on his hands.

The coach walked down the aisle and put his hand on Steve's shoulder.

"Have you anything to say to these fellows, Steve?"

Steve rose slowly, rubbing the sleeve of his jersey across his nose.

"I haven't much to say, Coach. I'm glad the cup is back. Skiffo and Larry and Big Bill got a little fouled up on it, that's all. I'll never hold it against them. I think they're swell guys, really, and I hope that we can be friends again."

"Time's up, Coach," Pete Slade said.

"Okay, fellows," Coach Hartford said. "The same team that was playing at the end of the half will take the field. On your way."

The players filed out of the room. Once again Steve Morgan came last, but this time he was walking on clouds. The trophy was back. Skiffo, Larry and Big Bill had apologized. When he came out of the tunnel he found the world a different place. The sunshine was glorious. The air was wonderful. Bert Logan was still playing in his position, but that made little difference to Steve. He felt exhilarated, full of life. He took his place on the end of the substitutes' bench, and filled his lungs with fresh air. It was good to be alive, good to be here in this big stadium.

He wondered how Yogi had engineered the return of the trophy. When he found that little freckle-faced freshman he would squeeze a confession out of him.

Just then Steve felt a tug on the sleeve of his sweater. He looked around. Yogi was squatting on the turf at his side, hugging a camera that was almost as big as he was.

"Yogi!" Steve exclaimed. "You're just the fellow I'm looking for. The trophy is back."

Yogi grinned.

"How did you do it?" Steve asked.

"Promise you'll never tell?"

Steve nodded.

"Penny really figured it out," Yogi explained.

"Penny?"

"Yeah. She suspected Blink Kennedy because he took a swing at you in the Beanery. She found out he had joined the Wallingford Owls before he left old Central. They meet every week in Blink's basement. We played a hunch and went to Blink's house on a meeting night. We peeked in a window, and there was the All-city Cup sitting on the table, big as life."

"But how did you get them to return it?"

"I'm coming to that. Blink and the other members were holding a meeting around that table. While they were singing we raised the window carefully and put my flashlight camera on the sill. We had to work fast, but we got the picture. The rest was simple. We developed several prints and mailed one to each member of the club. We sent a typewritten note with the picture telling them that if they failed to return the cup by today, the picture would be turned over to the newspapers and the police."

" 'We?' " Steve asked. "Was Penny in on all this?"

"I'll say she was," Yogi answered, grinning. "We used her car for the getaway. She kept the motor running while I took the picture."

"Yogi," Steve said, "I could kiss you!"

"Oh, no!" Yogi said, drawing away. "Not that!"

The second half of the Portside-State game had started, but Steve had been so intent on getting the story from Yogi that he had paid little attention to it.

Portside had received on the twenty-yard line, and Skiffo had carried the ball back to the thirty-five. On the third play of the second half, Syd Johnson ran into trouble. He twisted his leg in a pile-up, and had to be carried from the game. They placed him on the substitute bench, and Coach Hartford inspected his ankle to see if it was fractured.

"I'll be all right, Coach," Syd said, "but Skiffo wanted me to tell you they need Steve Morgan in there."

Steve overheard the remark, and his heart started to pound. Skiffo Drake wanted him in the game. That meant that Larry Bowman and Big Bill wanted him too.

Coach Hartford turned to Steve.

"Replace Bert Logan," he said.

Steve bounded from the bench and raced out on the field. He hardly heard the cheer from the Portside stands. He was interested in only one thing—getting his hands on that ball.

Skiffo ran Larry Bowman off tackle, giving Portside a first down on the forty-eight. Then he called for time out. It was an unusual thing to do. The linemen looked up, surprised, and they were even more surprised when Skiffo Drake, Larry Bowman, Big Bill Toner, and Steve Morgan went into a little huddle off to one side. It was apparent that the linemen were not in on this.

The four backfield men locked hands, and Skiffo started to speak.

"You heard what we said in the locker room, Steve. We mean it—every word of it. We played like a bunch of quarreling baboons in that first half. But this half is going to be different. This half we're going to play like the *Rambling Rams* from old Central. Isn't that right, Larry?"

"Right," Larry replied.

"How about it, Bill?"

"It's a deal," Big Bill Toner said.

"Are you with us, Steve?"

"All the way," Steve said, his heart bubbling over with joy.

"Okay," Skiffo said, tightening his grip. "They closed old Central, but they didn't kill the spirit of old Central. It's right here. This is old Central High. There are a lot of grads up there in the stands. Let's tuck this one away for them."

Coach Hartford stood on the sidelines and watched that tight little huddle. He had no way of knowing what was going on there, but he had a hunch, and he wasn't wrong.

On the next play Big Bill Toner took the ball and, following a ripping, smashing interference that opened a hole a mile wide, went plowing through, thundering toward the goal. He crossed the State forty, the thirty-five, the thirty, before Butch Hogan pulled him down.

In the huddle Skiffo, Larry, Bill and Steve grinned at one another.

"Twenty-six," Skiffo said. That was Steve's signal.

Steve hit the line like a jet-propelled bomber. His pounding feet dug into the turf. Spinning, twisting, whirling, he fought his way down to the twenty.

"Okay, Larry, it's your turn. Twenty-two. Got it?" The line nodded. They sensed that something had happened to this backfield—some kind of miracle that was beyond their understanding. But whatever it was, the linemen were all for it. The blue-clad team of Portside came out of the huddle with the click and precision of a drill team.

Larry Bowman, with shoulders down and sturdy legs flashing, was dynamite on two feet. He blasted through the line, spun around like a top, and streaked off on a slant. When they nailed him he was on the five-yard line.

State called for time.

"Got 'em worried." Skiffo grinned. "They don't know what they're up against."

The referee signalled that time was in.

Portside went into a huddle. Skiffo looked at Big Bill. "How about sixteen?"

Big Bill nodded.

Sixteen was right over the middle, and that's where Big Bill went. Harry Cowan was backing up the line for State, and when Big Bill's head hit him in the stomach, he sat down and slid for six feet on the seat of his pants.

The referee's hands flew into the air. Portside had scored. The crowd in the stadium went wild.

Here was a new Portside team. The fans sensed it.

Whatever it was that had happened during the half, it had turned this team into a smashing, powerful, amazing eleven.

In the radio booth an announcer was babbling into a microphone.

"I don't know what has come over this Portside team, folks, but believe me something new has been added. It's hard to believe it after that first half, but here it is right before my eyes. Portside is packing a brand new wallop —a terrific punch. They're lining up for the kick. Big Bill Toner is back. There goes the ball. There goes the kick. Right between the uprights, folks, and the score is now STATE 19, PORTSIDE 7."

Portside kicked off to State. Bob Reed took it on the ten, but he was bottled up by Erickson and Mallet.

The Portside line, encouraged by the new life in the backfield, was buckling down. State made three attempts and gained only six yards. They kicked on the fourth, and Skiffo took the ball on the mid-field stripe. Steve and Big Bill cleared a path for him, and he was back to the thirty-eight before they downed him.

Portside opened up on this drive. They threw passes all over the place, and when they had the State defense spread out, they clipped off big gains through the line. Drake, Bowman, Toner, and Morgan punched, dove, fought, and squirmed their way down the field. Over the thirty! Over the twenty! Over the ten!

In the huddle Skiffo called for a reverse—Bowman to Morgan. Steve took it on the fly and started for the sideline. Halfway there he saw an opening. With a quick change of pace he shot through the hole and went over standing up. Portside had scored again.

Instead of kicking on this try-for-point, Skiffo shot a quick pass to Erickson right behind the line. It was good for the extra point.

The eyes of the crowd were on the scoreboard when the numbers changed: STATE 19, PORTSIDE 14.

On the sidelines Coach Hartford was walking up and down, a big grin on his face. What more could a coach ask for? There was a backfield that really clicked.

State took possession of the ball early in the third quarter and managed to keep it for a good share of the time. Their offense had stiffened, and for a time they looked like a threat, but Butch Hogan fumbled on the thirty-yard line and Steve Morgan leaped for the ball, wrapping his arms around it.

This was the break they had been waiting for. Portside worked it down to the fifty and had to kick, but it put State with their backs to the goal line. They brought it out, but it was a long, slow process. Where they had made eight and ten yards before they now made only three and four. Doggedly they hung on, and Skiffo glanced at the scoreboard. There were five minutes left.

"Get your hands on that ball," he kept repeating. "We can't score without the ball."

State kicked from the forty-eight, and Larry took it on the thirty. He hammered his way down to the thirty-five, the forty, where Bob Reed forced him out of bounds.

When the ball was brought in, Portside gathered for the signals. Skiffo looked around at the sweat-streaked faces.

"This is it, gang," he said. "This is where we wrap it up."

He called for number forty-two. Forty-two was a reverse with a shovel pass. It went around the left side of the line, with Larry packing the oval.

The Portside team moved into position.

Wagner snapped the ball to Skiffo. Skiffo whirled, faked it to Steve, and shoveled it to Larry, who was running wide. The guards had come out for interference, and with Big Bill Toner leading the way, they smashed around end. Toner took Young off his feet, and the path was wide open for Bowman.

Skiffo had streaked through the line, and he put a rolling block on Earl Nevers. They went down in a pile, Skiffo throwing his weight on top of the State halfback, who was squirming to get free.

While Larry was pounding down the left sideline, Steve had circled the right end and was cutting back across the field. He was heading for Bob Reed, hoping to take him out of the play, but Reed was moving like a scared jackrabbit in an effort to nail Bowman. It was a race between Steve and Reed, and it appeared that Reed would win.

Larry Bowman sensed this, and just before Reed hit him, he whirled and flipped the ball back in a lateral to Steve. Steve juggled it for a moment on his finger-tips, and then pulled it to his chest without breaking his stride.

Stan Williams, who had been blocked out by a tackle, had wiggled free and was racing across the field in Steve's direction. Steve slanted away from him, but he could see that Williams was gaining.

He saw Williams leave the ground, felt his hands slap the thigh pads in his pants. At the same instant Steve spun on his toes. Like a whirling dervish, he broke the hold that Williams was trying to get. With his cleats digging into the sod, Steve started in another direction. Three linemen were thundering down on him, but Steve found new power pumping into his legs.

He could hear the crowd screeching in the stands. He could hear the heavy breathing behind him, the pounding feet. He gave it a little more . . . a burst of speed . . . a little more. This one was for old Central. This one was for Laurel High. This one was for the *Rambling Rams*. This one was for Yogi Zimmerman.

Wasn't that Yogi Zimmerman crouched behind the goal post, his camera raised? There was a flash of white light when Steve's cleats crossed the last marker. A tackler hit him, but it was too late. Steve went down behind the goal line with both arms hugging the ball tight against his body.

When the game was over, Steve walked to the tunnel with Skiffo, Larry, and Big Bill Toner.

"What are you doing tonight?" Skiffo asked.

"I'm going to the Tolo Dance with Penny Carson."

"Great! How about meeting us before the dance. We'll make it a party. It'll be the first annual reunion of the *Rambling Rams*."

Arm in arm they disappeared into the tunnel that led to the dressing rooms. The Phantom Backfield was together again.